Reckoning

Ms Vengeance Book 1

Ken Preston

MY CREATIVE WRITING LIFE

Copyright © 2021 by Ken Preston

All rights reserved.

No portion of this book may be reproduced in any form without written permission from the publisher or author, except as permitted by U.S. copyright law.

Contents

Chapter 1	1
Chapter 2	10
Chapter 3	23
Chapter 4	29
Chapter 5	40
Chapter 6	45
Chapter 7	55
Chapter 8	63
Chapter 9	81
Chapter 10	89
Chapter 11	98
Chapter 12	108
Chapter 13	122
Chapter 14	140

Chapter 15	150
Chapter 16	160
Chapter 17	167
Chapter 18	170
Chapter 19	175
Chapter 20	177
Chapter 21	181
Chapter 22	184
Chapter 23	197
Chapter 24	199
Chapter 25	202
Chapter 26	213
Chapter 27	220
Chapter 28	222
Chapter 29	238
Acknowledgements	241
Joe Coffin	243
Joe Coffin Chapter One	245
Writing in the Shadows	261

Chapter 1

His job was killing people, but that didn't mean he couldn't appreciate culture and fine art.

He wasn't a monster.

His fingers ran over the piano keys, and he closed his eyes as he played.

Mozart's Eine Kleine Nachtmusik. A favourite of his, one that comforted him and reminded him of home and his mother. She often played this piece on their grand piano. At least, that's how he remembered his childhood. He could even remember dancing and jumping up and down, laughing with delight. He didn't have many memories of his mother. She died in the same conflagration that destroyed the Blüthner, when he was still very young.

He'd had little hope that he could coax even the most basic of tunes out of this monstrosity when he first saw it. The upright piano was chipped and scratched, its top stained with coffee rings, and the keys yellowed with age and greasy with thousands of fingerprints. The acoustics here at Euston train station were appalling, and even the most skilled of pianists would have trouble competing with the sounds of the crowded concourses, the tannoy announcements, and the hiss of coffee machines. And yet he hadn't been able to resist sitting down and playing when it became free.

He'd had to stand and wait while the two brats, fighting for space on the wooden chair, had pounded at the keys. Their mother had looked on adoringly, and he'd had to fight the impulse to push the children off the chair and stamp on their faces.

He'd had to remind himself he wasn't a monster.

The mother must have seen something in his face, some inkling of the horror he could wreak if he had less self-control. She had grown uneasy and urged her children to get down from the public piano and let the man take his turn. He'd given her a smile of gratitude, which she briefly returned before hurrying her two children away and into the crowd.

Now, as he played, he wondered about the idea of these pianos placed in public spaces. What was the point? Was it an attempt to foster 'good old-fashioned values' amongst the populace? Perhaps it was expected that once someone sat down and began playing, a crowd would gather. Maybe even burst into song.

Pathetic. The worker drones were too busy rushing from one job to the next to pause long enough to even notice the piano, let alone appreciate it. They ran for their trains or hurried through barriers and down steps deep underground for the tube trains. And let them.

Work. Watch TV. Sleep.

Keep busy.

Don't think.

Don't pause long enough to realise that the world was dying around them.

'You are exceptional on there.'

He paused, his fingers hovering over the piano keys, and looked up at the speaker. An old man, wearing a shirt and tie and a trilby. Dark patches of sweat had formed beneath his armpits, and there was a slight sheen on his forehead.

'Thank you. I see it's looking like another hot day outside.'

The old man smiled and nodded. 'At least it's a relief from all that rain we had last week, although I'm told there's more on the way. The weather makes no sense anymore. I'm old enough that I can remember when it used to snow in winter and sunshine in summer. Now I never know what season we are in unless I check a calendar.'

He nodded. 'And yet despite all the rain we have, the government still tells us to ration our water usage, as there is a drought. It hardly makes any sense, does it?'

The old man pulled a handkerchief out of his pocket and mopped his brow. 'Nothing makes any sense, my friend. When you reach my age, you'll realise that.'

He gestured at the piano. 'Do you play?'

'Yes, every day I come down here and play. I tune it as well and look after it as best I can, although as you can see, it is in dreadful condition.'

'I wondered how it had managed to stay in tune. You are obviously very generous with your time.'

'I like to think that I bring some cheer and happiness into people's lives.' The old man shrugged. 'But I probably just annoy everyone.'

He stood up and stepped to one side. 'Please, take a seat, play.'

'Oh no, I didn't intend to interrupt you, you were playing so beautifully.'

'Please sit down and play, I promise you're not interrupting me.' He glanced up at the departure board, at the clock. 'I have to go, anyway.'

'Thank you, you're very kind.' The old man eased himself onto the chair with a heavy sigh. He removed his hat and placed it on top of the piano.

'Let me hear you play before I go.'

'Oh, I'm nowhere near as skilled as you, I just tinkle around a little.'

The old man placed his fingers on the keys and began playing.

The tune was familiar, but he couldn't place it. The old man was better than he gave himself credit for. He glanced at the clock again.

'It was a pleasure meeting you, but I really do have to go now.'

'And you, young man, and you.' The old man spoke without looking up or stopping playing. 'Take care, my friend.'

He walked away and left the old man playing. The cheerful tune struggled to compete with the hustle and bustle of Euston Station. Soon it was lost to him as he pushed his way through the barrier and took the steps underground.

He found the Victoria Line and stood on the platform, waiting. Less than a minute later and the familiar wave of warm air rushed over him as a train approached. It erupted from the tunnel, brakes squealing as it slowed to a halt. The doors opened, commuters spilling out and pressing against the crush of people trying to get on.

He stayed where he was.

It wasn't time.

Ten minutes later and his quarry arrived, just as he had predicted. He had spent the last two weeks observing Simon Revel-Humphrey's movements and habits. His working hours, his commuter route, his eating and drinking routines. There could be no suspicion of foul play about this man's death, they had made that perfectly clear.

That ruled out the obvious method: a bullet to the head, always his preferred option. Especially on those rare occasions when he was allowed to get up close to his victim, with no danger of discovery. He liked to give his prey a moment to realise what was about to happen before he pulled the trigger. He enjoyed seeing their expression transform from confusion to horror as they realised these were their last living moments.

Nothing else compared.

Still, an assignment like this had its pleasures. There was the challenge to begin with; how to kill someone without raising suspicion? There were several options, but after trailing his quarry for these last two weeks, he had settled on one.

Revel-Humphrey boarded the next train to arrive at the platform.

He followed.

All the seats had been taken, and the aisle was full of people standing. Revel-Humphrey stood only three feet away, one hand clutching a handrail and the other a coffee cup. The briefcase he carried everywhere sat between his feet on the carriage floor. Revel-Humphrey liked to drink coffee. The reusable travel cup bore a sustainability logo on the side.

Revel-Humphrey was an ethical coffee consumer.

He chuckled at that. Was there anything ethical about this man's life?

When they arrived at the station, Revel-Humphrey left the train, as he had predicted.

He followed his quarry, gaining on him as they approached the long escalator to the surface.

He had to time this just right.

As the escalator reached the top, he pushed past Revel-Humphrey, knocking his elbow and tipping the coffee cup out of his hand. The cup hit the floor, and the lid fell off. Milky coffee splashed across the station tiles.

'I am so sorry!' he said.

Revel-Humphrey pushed his glasses back onto the bridge of his nose and simply stood where he was as impatient travellers swarmed around him, rushing for their next connection. He was a sallow, slight man, the kind who sprints into middle-age, having done nothing more than sit in an office all his working life.

'Let me buy you another drink.' He stooped and picked up the cup and the lid. White coffee puddled in the indent of a broken floor tile.

'No, that's quite all right.' Revel-Humphrey reached out for the cup.

'No, I absolutely insist. That was deplorable of me.' He kept hold of the cup, holding it close as though it belonged to him now.

Revel-Humphrey laughed nervously. 'No, I can see you are in a hurry, it's quite all right, honestly.'

He began walking. 'There's a coffee cart down here, one

of those quaint looking things, but they have all the mod cons. What were you drinking, cappuccino was it?'

Revel-Humphrey trotted after him. 'I don't want to put you to any trouble!'

'No trouble at all, it's the least I can do.'

He took long, fast strides across the concourse. Revel-Humphrey had to break into a run to keep up with him.

He reached the coffee stand, all made up to appear like an old-fashioned, ornate gypsy caravan, in contrast to the interior filled with modern chrome gadgetry.

He placed the cup and the lid on the counter. 'Would you mind giving these a rinse? I'm afraid I dropped it on the floor. And then a cappuccino, please.'

Revel-Humphrey, slightly breathless and with a reddish glow to his cheeks, arrived at the coffee stand. 'Please, it's quite—'

'Quite all right, yes I know!' He laughed. 'It's too late now, I've ordered your drink and I will be most offended if you don't accept it by way of an apology.'

With his index finger, Revel-Humphrey pushed his glasses back onto the bridge of his nose. 'Well, thank you, that's very generous of you.'

He paid with his phone whilst the chrome coffee machine dispensed the drink.

After giving the coffee cup lid a quick rinse, the barista placed it on the counter. Droplets of water clung to the smooth plastic.

He took a square of paper towel and picked up the lid. He dried it thoroughly and handed it to Revel-Humphrey.

'Thank you.' Revel-Humphrey repeatedly turned the lid over in his hands whilst waiting for his drink.

'Look, I must go, I'm late as it is. Apologies once again.'
'Oh, no need.'

He was already walking away, taking those long, swift strides across the concourse.

He didn't look back once.

He found the public toilets and entered. Once inside and on his own, he removed his jacket, balled it up and stuffed it in a waste bin. The jacket was now contaminated and fit only for disposal. It didn't matter, he had another one waiting for him in a locker at Southwark Station.

He washed his hands under hot water, scrubbing at them and applying liberal amounts of soap. He'd brought his own supply of soap, you never could be sure that the public toilets would have any, but he had no need of it. Once he was satisfied that his hands were clean, he dried them under the hand dryer and then stepped back onto the concourse.

No sign of his victim.

He hoped Revel-Humphrey would enjoy his coffee. It was almost certainly his last. Within a few hours, he would start to feel nauseous. Shortly after that, he would suffer blurred vision and then facial weakness. His speech would become slurred and he would begin having difficulty breathing. Within two days at the most, he would be dead.

Once his symptoms grew severe enough, he would, of course, seek medical help. The hospital may even diagnose botulism and begin treatment, but it would be too late. The dose of botulinum toxin that he had smeared across Revel-Humphrey's coffee cup lid when he was drying it had been far higher than the necessary lethal threshold.

A thousand nanograms per kilogram of body weight was enough. For Revel-Humphrey, that would be about 70,000 nanograms, or 0.00007 of a gram.

He had smeared one hundred times that amount over the lid; the toxin suspended in a tasteless, invisible paste of his own design and contained within a plastic, breakable vial in his jacket pocket. Even if Revel-Humphrey didn't drink through the lid, he had enough of it on his fingers after handling it that at some point he would ingest it by touching his mouth, eyes or nose.

It was quite probable that he would spread enough of it around by touching various surfaces on his way home that he would infect many other people, too. There would be a localised public health emergency declared once the outbreak of botulism had been identified. Several innocents would die.

He headed back to the underground.

The day had only just begun, but already he was awash with a tremendous sense of accomplishment.

CHAPTER 2

OLIVER SCREAMED. ONE OF his wine-glass-shattering, ear-bleeding specials. He was staring at the television, a muscle in his neck twitching, his Adam's Apple bobbing up and down as though he might be about to throw up. Amber the cat who had been curled up next to him on the sofa, leapt onto the floor and dashed out of the living room.

Maddie looked at the television to see what had upset him. A clip of Edward Porter, leader of the political party British Values, leaving his offices with his aide walking beside him, shielding him from the mob of reporters with microphones and cameras. Both men wore a shirt and tie and tailored jackets, and yet to Maddie they were just thugs, hard men playing at being politicians.

The news report cut back to the studio, the presenter sitting on a settee with Porter sat at the other end.

'Thank you for joining us this morning, Mr Porter. Let's get right to the matter at hand and the statement you made yesterday that we played in that clip. That's quite a controversial thing to say, don't you think?'

Maddie pulled the TV remote out of Oliver's hand and hit the power off switch. The screen died and turned black.

Oliver threw his head back and screamed again.

Maddie turned her back on him, flung the remote onto the sofa, and stalked into the kitchen. When he got like this, it was best just to ignore him. She slammed the dishwasher door shut with more force than was necessary. It began humming as the wash cycle began, along with that ticking noise that had never been there before last week and said that there was something wrong in the machine's guts and it wouldn't last much longer.

'Mum? Where's my blazer?'

Maddie took a deep breath and turned around to face her daughter. 'It's exactly where you threw it last night when you got in from school.'

'Yeah, but where? I've looked everywhere and I'm going to be late.'

Maddie didn't reply. She couldn't. The sight of her teenage daughter, fifteen next month, had rendered Maddie speechless.

'Mum?'

Maddie blinked and gave her head a tiny shake. 'Oh, sorry, I was just wondering how on earth you're going to explain your absence from school today to the headteacher.'

Jessica put that look on her face, the one that said, you're making absolutely no sense, and I really don't have time for this. 'What are you talking about? I'm going to school.'

'Not dressed like that, you're not.' Maddie pointed at Jessica's skirt. 'That tiny scrap of material desperately trying to be a skirt barely covers your butt cheeks. Go and get changed.'

'Mum!'

Oliver screamed again. Maddie heard voices talking. He had switched the television back on.

Jessica rolled her eyes. 'Mum, the skirt is fine.'

'No, it's not, change into another one.'

'But, Mum—'

'I said change your skirt.'

Jessica glared at her mother. Maddie glared back.

'Fine!' Jessica turned and stomped out of the kitchen. Her school skirt, which had once been the required length, bounced with her movements and briefly revealed a hint of Jessica's underwear. She must have taken the skirt up with her friend Eve. Ever since Maddie had dragged her children up here, away from everyone and everything they knew, she'd been desperate for Jessica to make new friends. But now that Jessica had finally made a friend, Maddie found herself wishing that it had been anyone but that girl Eve.

Maddie hoped that Jessica had only altered the one skirt.

Amber's tail tickled Maddie's ankles as she snaked between them.

'You can stop that right now,' Maddie said. 'I've already fed you this morning.'

Oliver screamed again.

Maddie stomped back into the living room. *Seriously, Oliver? Do you really have to be acting up right now?*

Oliver scowled at his mother, eyebrows scrunched together and his cheeks glowing with two red spots.

Something was upsetting him, that was for sure.

Maddie looked at the TV. Edward Porter was still being interviewed.

'No, Dianne, that's not right, we are not a racist party at all, and we have a record of upholding values and respect for all coloured people.'

She turned back to Oliver. 'What? You're obviously upset about something, so tell me.'

Oliver continued glowering up at Maddie. He was sitting on his spot on the sofa, the one he always sat in. After two years, the cushion had a dip in it, the fabric a slight sheen. But then the sofa had been secondhand when Maddie bought it. All of their furniture from their previous house had been too big to fit in this tiny cottage.

'But Diane, my point is that the adoption of critical race theory into our culture was catastrophic for the UK, and that the idea that there are under-represented sections of society in Britain, the most tolerant and least racist country in the world, is ridiculous.'

A game controller lay on the cushion beside Oliver, next to the remote. The twelve-year-old had his strict routines and one of the most important was playing on the Xbox before the day's home-schooling began.

This morning he hadn't switched the console on. Instead, he was watching the breakfast news on BBC1, and was obviously very upset about something.

'All right, let's move on. Your party's stance on climate change has more than raised a few eyebrows in the scientific community. Aren't we long past the point of arguing that man-made climate change is real and happening right now?'

Still staring at the television, Oliver let rip with another ear-piercing scream.

'Of course we are, and that's not what I was saying at all. My point is that our current government is throwing money away, millions of pounds, hundreds of millions, which could be put to much better use.'

'So you disagree with the money that has been spent on the new Thames Barrier?'

Maddie battled the urge to scream back at Oliver, to see how he liked that.

'The three billion and counting that has been thrown at this vanity project by our Prime Minister could have been used to fund our NHS and cut taxes for the hardworking families of the UK. It is utterly disgusting—'

'You don't agree then that Londoners need protection from potential flooding now that the old Thames Barrier has been declared no longer fit for purpose?'

Maybe an attempt at diplomacy might work. That's what Ellie said. *You're too hard on him. He suffered a terrible trauma. He needs time to work it through. He'll talk again, one day.*

'I would say our cash-strapped NHS is no longer fit for purpose, wouldn't you, Diane? And this is our promise to voters, that we will cut out the cancer of corruption and back-handed deals and we will spend the taxpayers' money where it is needed, starting with our NHS.'

Maddie squatted beside Oliver, lowered her voice to what she hoped was a soothing tone. 'Come on, Oliver, what's wrong?' She placed a hand over his. He snatched it away.

Maddie stood up. 'Fine.' She turned her back on him and stalked out of the living room, unconsciously mimicking her teenage daughter's actions of only a minute ago.

Back in the kitchen, Maddie leaned on the sink and gazed out of the window; a small square set deep into the recess in the thick cottage wall. It didn't let much light in.

But the view was breathtaking. Green fields rolled away to Ladhar Bheinn mountain in the distance, a dense forest at its base. The hard blue of the sky promised yet another day of intolerable heat and relentless sunshine.

Apparently it would soon be raining back in London, back where Maddie had once lived in what felt like another life now. The familiar spike of pain ran through her chest as Maddie thought of the other house, the family house, the house in which her children had been supposed to grow up in, the house they had been happy in.

Before The Thing happened, the thing that nobody mentioned anymore. That nobody had talked about in a long time. If not for The Thing That Happened, they wouldn't be here in the Highlands of Scotland, about as far away from London as Maddie had been able to flee with her two remaining children without having to move abroad.

This wasn't how her life had meant to play out. A single mother to two children.

One rebellious teenage daughter, which was par for the course, really.

And a mute, autistic twelve-year-old boy, which wasn't.

Maddie took a deep, ragged breath. Gripped the edges of the Belfast sink, the white china cold beneath her hands.

Dank despair flowed through her, filling her chest and head.

Well done, Maddie, you've opened the floodgates now, haven't you? How many times have I told you, don't stop, don't even pause, just keep moving?

The memories caught up with her when she stopped moving, even for a moment. Memories of her husband

and youngest boy, murdered in their home. Jonathon and Harry both stabbed to death in a methamphetamine-fuelled, frenzied knife attack. Harry had been six. Maddie screwed her eyes shut. She wouldn't let the tears come, not now.

'Mum?'

Maddie opened her eyes and turned around.

'Oh, Mum.' Jessica approached her mum and wrapped her arms around her, burying her head in her chest.

Maddie held her daughter briefly and then let go. 'All right, come on, I'm fine. You need to go or you'll be late.'

Jessica stepped back, pushed her long hair off her face. Gave her mum another look, but this one was harder to interpret.

'You are allowed to cry sometimes, you know,' Jessica said.

She picked up her school rucksack, turned her back on her mother and left the kitchen. She slammed the front door as she left the cottage.

Wait, we didn't say goodbye properly. Maddie considered running to the door, flinging it open and shouting after Jessica. Had Jessica remembered that her mother wouldn't be here later, once she came home from school?

Maddie's sister, Ellie, appeared in the kitchen doorway. 'Wow, you lot certainly know how to start your day off, don't you?' Wearing crumpled pyjamas, she looked as though she had just climbed out of bed.

'I'm sorry, we woke you, didn't we?'

Running her fingers through her tangled hair, Ellie padded barefoot across the kitchen and straight for the coffee percolator. 'No, not really, and I needed to get up anyway, I'd been in bed far too long. It was that epic journey yesterday, it exhausted me. Five trains, one bus, a boat and a ride in a broken down old Land Rover. All that was missing was a camel ride and a trek into the jungle.' Ellie yawned. 'Does your day always start with screaming and door slamming?'

'They won't be like this for you, they love their Aunt Ellie.'

'I don't know, they seem pretty stressed.' Ellie poured herself a coffee. 'You think maybe it might be better for them if they were, y'know, living somewhere there are people around?'

'There are people here.' Already Maddie could feel her chest tightening with tension. How many times had they had this conversation already? Endless hours spent on the phone as Ellie attempted to persuade her sister to return to London. More hours lost after each phonecall as Maddie cried quietly, wishing she could have her life back.

'You know what I'm saying, Maddie. Poor Jess has to be driven by Land Rover down to the harbour where she takes a boat over to the mainland and a bus to the school. That's no life for a teenager.'

'None of the other kids at her school mind.'

'They've never known anything different. Jess should be back in London, out with her friends, not cooped up in this rabbit hutch in the back end of nowhere.'

Maddie slammed the flat of her hand on the kitchen counter, rattling a stand of dishes. 'Will you just stop? I didn't ask you here to criticise my parenting skills.'

A seagull cried out overhead, filling the silence in the kitchen. From the lounge came the sounds of talking on the television.

'That's not fair, Maddie, you know I'm not criticising you. What you've been through, losing Jonathon and Harry like that, was just awful. I just don't think it's good for you all, hiding here, it's not good for you or the children.'

'Well thank you for your advice, but I think I am quite capable of deciding what's best for us.'

Ellie held up her hands in a show of surrender. 'I know you are, Maddie.'

Maddie took a deep breath. 'I'm sorry I didn't mean to snap at you.'

Ellie sipped at her coffee. 'Bob sends his regards and wants to know when you're coming down to London and visit him and Mary.'

'You didn't tell him, did you?'

'No, your secret's safe with me.' Ellie sipped her coffee again. 'Although, to be honest, he's going to be upset when he finds out you were in town and didn't call on them.'

'I told you, it's going to be a busy couple of days, I won't have time.'

'Yeah, I get that, but couldn't you just—'

'Will you stop trying to run my life for me!'

A silence hung between the sisters, only the murmur of the television from the lounge and the cry of the seagulls outside disturbing the fragility.

Maddie turned her back on Ellie and walked into the lounge, her legs stiff like sticks of wood and her shoulders bunched with knots of tension.

Oliver was still watching television, but the presenters had moved on from the interview and were now discussing the California wildfires.

'Whipped by sixty mile-per-hour winds, the fire has burned through seventy-six thousand acres of forest and destroyed over one thousand homes and other buildings. Middletown in Lake County has been evacuated, and there are reports that four people have lost their lives.'

Those splodges of anger were still visible on Oliver's cheeks, but he seemed to have calmed down. At least he had stopped screaming.

'Oliver, turn off the TV and come into the kitchen.'

Oliver looked at his mother. His eyes were damp with tears that hadn't quite fallen. Over the last couple of weeks he had been agitated and upset. During the nights Maddie had woken up to hear him padding around his bedroom, the creak of the uneven wooden floorboards like a metronome ticking out the endless hours until the dawn. Some nights Maddie had considered asking him what was wrong, why couldn't he sleep? But the thought of standing in his bedroom doorway, head bowed below the low door frame, waiting for him to speak when she knew he wouldn't, always stopped her.

'Turn the television off, Oliver.'

And why have you been watching the news? she wanted to ask. *I can't believe you have a sudden interest in politics.*

Oliver continued staring blank-faced at Maddie.

'Oliver, it's time for your lessons, so you need to turn off the television and come into the kitchen.'

The same routine every morning. Except this morning the backdrop to Maddie's one-sided conversation was political commentary and the news instead of the theme music to Lego Batman on the Xbox. When Oliver had made up his mind about something and reality intruded to disrupt that, Maddie knew it took a few minutes for him to process the change. She had a certain sympathy with him, but she couldn't let that influence her day. Not when she had a timetable to keep to. The Land Rover to the harbour, the boat across to the mainland and the bus to the train station.

'Oliver.' Maddie raised the level of her voice a notch to show that she was losing patience. 'Turn off the television.'

Oliver jabbed his forefinger at Maddie and then with his palm flat and fingers outstretched, he placed his fingertips against his chin and moved his hand away and down.

Maddie sighed. Of course, she had forgotten to ask politely.

'Oliver, *please* turn off the television and come into the kitchen.'

He picked up the remote and the TV screen turned dark and silent.

Back in the kitchen, Ellie was sitting at the table and drinking her coffee. 'Morning Ollie, how's my favourite nephew?'

Oliver glanced at Ellie and then sat down at the table. Another second-hand item, the tabletop was scarred with scuff marks, stains, initials scratched into the wood, and one scorch mark.

Maddie laid out his schoolbooks. Oliver glared at them like they might leap up and bite him.

Maddie turned away and pulled open the back door. Already the day was heating up and soon the tiny kitchen would be stifling. She stood in the open doorway and gazed at the shoreline and the green water of Loch Nevis.

Took a deep breath to calm herself. Across the bay she could just make out the white of the schoolhouse and the houses scattered along the street.

'I should get going,' she said.

'What time do you get in?'

Maddie turned back to face her sister. 'I arrive at Euston at seven tonight.'

'You want Martin to pick you up? The spare bedroom is all ready and waiting for you.'

They'd already had this conversation, but Maddie had known she would have to endure it again.

'No, like I said already, I'm fine, thank you.'

'Maddie, I'm really proud of you for doing this, it can't be easy going back—'

'I'm not going back to the house!' Maddie snapped her mouth shut, regretting the sharpness of her voice.

'I know, Maddie, but still, it's a big thing.' Ellie reached out her hand and took Maddie's, squeezing lightly. 'You're going to be great, you know that, don't you?'

Words of gratitude jammed in Maddie's chest, even as her stomach twisted with guilt for the lies she had told her sister. Maddie simply nodded. The beep of a horn rescued her from having to say anything.

'Sounds like my lift down to the harbour.'

Ellie sighed and stood up, held out her arms in an invitation to embrace. 'Come here.'

The sisters hugged.

Maddie said goodbye to Oliver.

'Be good for Aunt Ellie, okay?'

Oliver nodded.

'I'll be back Thursday evening,' Maddie said to her sister, and hoisted the backpack over her shoulders.

Ellie smiled. 'Don't worry about us, we're going to have fun.'

Maddie nodded and stepped outside. A warm breeze ruffled her hair as she climbed the footpath to the waiting Land Rover.

If Maddie had known she was never returning, she might have paused to take in the beauty of her surroundings one final time. Paused to soak up the solitude and the endless sky.

Instead, she climbed into the back of the Land Rover.

The taxi driver slammed the door shut.

Maddie settled into her seat, the rucksack beside her. She was relieved to have escaped her sister's prying eyes. Maddie had refused to tell Ellie the reason for her trip to London. Ellie had eventually decided that it must be for a job interview, and that her little sister didn't want to jinx the outcome by revealing too much about it.

The truth was far more mysterious, a meeting with the former Minister for the Environment, Simon Revel-Humphrey. A man she had no previous connection with, but who'd been most insistent that they meet.

The only reason she had finally agreed to his request was his revelation that it involved Jonathon.

And that was all he would say.

Chapter 3

Spider slapped at the hand creeping up her inner thigh. When that didn't stop him, she grabbed his skinny wrist and yanked it off.

'Aww, come on!' Dean leaned in close, his hand back on her thigh, his nicotine breath in her face.

'Fuck off, Dean!'

'None of that language in my house, young lady.' Dean's father stood in the living room doorway, a cigarette dangling from between his lips. Spider had never seen him without a smoke. The endless chain of cigarettes stuck to his lips were a part of his features. Like someone who wore glasses taking them off, it would be weird seeing him without a fag in his mouth.

'Sorry, Mac.'

'I know the little bastard deserves it, but I won't have it, not in my house.' Mac turned his attention to Dean. 'And you leave that young lady alone, pawing over her like a sex-starved animal.'

'Dad!' Dean leaned back in the sofa. He had on a pair of skinny jeans and nothing else. His bare torso was covered in tattoos, skulls, Nazi insignia, naked women, swords. The tattoos ran up his neck and over his shaved skull.

'Where's Wayne? I told him to get your mother a cup of tea.'

'Where do you think? He's in the shitter.'

'Again?' Mac huffed. The cigarette between his lips trembled, sprinkling ash on his shirt. He brushed it off and ground it into the threadbare carpet with the sole of his slipper. 'Well, that's the khazi out of use for the rest of the afternoon.'

He shuffled out of the living room, presumably to get mother her cup of tea.

Mother sat in her usual chair in the opposite corner of the living room, wearing a shapeless dressing gown hanging from her thin, wasted body. Whenever Spider looked at her, which she tried to do as little as possible, the old woman nodded and grinned toothlessly back at her. She had to be the oldest woman Spider had ever seen. She never said a word, just nodded and grinned, and sometimes grunted with pleasure when she was eating her pureed food.

On a patched and stained sofa next to Mother's chair, Janis was painting her toenails a vivid red. Her long, greasy hair hung over her face, the tips almost brushing her toes as she concentrated. Janis was the youngest sibling, all skin and bone and a face like a heated argument.

Dean switched on the TV mounted to the wall and picked up a game controller. From the pout on his face, Spider guessed he'd fallen into a sulk. His thumbs jabbed at the controller as he shot zombies.

He'd been attempting to get Spider into bed for the last few days, but she was only letting him get so far before she slapped him back. It was driving him mad, and Spider was enjoying every minute of it. Every day she came around to the house, she exposed a little more flesh for him. Today she'd chosen a pair of shorts that rode high enough he could see where her buttocks met her thighs, and a crop top that just about worked as a bra. When Dean saw her, his eyes popped out on stalks and he grew extra arms that were all over her in a flash.

Spider just slapped him off.

There was absolutely no way on earth she was giving in to him. Besides his lack of hygiene, there was no telling what filthy infections he was carrying. But most of all, she hated the skinny bastard.

'Where's Wayne?'

This time it was Stu asking the question, standing in the doorway where Mac had just been. Stu was the eldest, and he liked everyone to know it. His cheeks were pink from the shave he'd just had and his hair was gelled into spikes. He wore a white shirt and a black tie and was fiddling with the knot.

'On the shitter,' Dean said without looking away from his game.

'Fuck's sake, I need a piss,' Stu muttered. 'Oi, Wayne, how long are you gonna be in there?'

'I don't know, do I?' Wayne shouted, his voice muffled by the closed door.

There was only one toilet in the tiny, terraced house, and that was downstairs.

'Where you goin', Stu?' Janis straightened her leg out and examined her toes.

'Fuckin' Scotland, and I'd like to have a piss before I spend the rest of the fuckin' day on the fuckin' motorway.'

'What you goin' to Scotland for, Stu?' Janis curled her leg up and began touching up her big toenail.

'Fuck's sake, Janis,' Stu muttered. 'Do you have to do that in here? That shit stinks.'

Janis ignored her brother and continued painting her toenails.

Someone banged on the front door.

'About fuckin' time,' Stu said, and went to answer the door.

'Aww, come on!' Dean shouted and threw the game controller across the tiny living room. A zombie filled the TV screen and then blood flew and splattered.

The game's controller thudded next to Janis on the sofa.

'You almost hit me in the head with that thing, you stupid prick!' Janis screamed.

'It might have knocked some sense into you.'

Janis launched herself at Dean with a guttural scream. The pot of red nail varnish hit the floor and scarlet splatters decorated the wall and the carpet. Spider scrambled out of the way as Janis punched and kicked Dean.

'Stop that now!' Mac yelled as he hobbled into the living room, tea slopping over the rim of a cup in his hand. 'Look what you made me do!'

'Dad, get her off me!' Dean yelled.

Janis pinched his nipple between her thumb and finger and twisted. Dean screamed and kicked out at Janis, but he couldn't get his leg up far enough to make contact. Laughing hysterically, Janis grabbed Dean between his legs and squeezed.

Dean screamed again. Mac threw the cup of tea over Janis, right in her face. She yelled and leapt off Dean.

'You scalded me!' she screamed, her hands to her face.

'Don't be stupid, you know your mother can only drink her tea lukewarm. Now sit down and behave yourself.'

A policeman walked into the living room, grinning. 'Morning, Mac.'

'Now, look at you, Terry, don't you look the part in that uniform.'

Janis collapsed onto the sofa, wailing from behind her hands clutching her face.

'Looks like you're having fun this morning.'

'Fuckin' bedlam as usual,' Stu said, entering the living room.

Spider backed up against the window. The room was too small for so many people, and she had begun to feel trapped and claustrophobic. She caught Terry eyeing her up and down.

'Don't worry, love, I'm not a real copper.'

'Yeah, whatever,' Spider said.

'What's your name then?'

'Spider.'

'Yeah? Why's that?'

'Why's what?'

'The name, love, what's with the name?'

Spider shrugged. 'Dunno.'

Terry grinned. Spider caught Dean staring at him. Terry obviously fancied himself as a ladies' man, and Dean didn't like the fact he was talking to his girlfriend.

'I should go,' Spider said. 'I've got to get to work. The manager said he'd fire me if I was late again.'

Terry grinned some more. 'You do that.' He turned to Stu. 'We should get going too, we've got a hell of a long drive ahead of us. I'm just going to have a piss first.'

'You can't,' Stu said. 'Wayne's in there.'

Terry chuckled. 'That boy should eat some fruit, get him regular like. All right, we'll stop off somewhere on the motorway. Bye, Mac.'

'Yeah, see you tonight,' Stu said.

The two men left.

Spider looked at Dean, who was massaging his balls. 'I'll see you later, yeah?'

Dean muttered something and cast a vicious glance at Janis, who was still sitting on the sofa with her hands over her face. At least she had stopped wailing.

'By, Mac.' Spider stepped over the puddle of tea on the carpet.

Outside, the sun's rays hit her like a physical blow. She watched as Stu and Terry drove away.

Terry gave her the creeps. It didn't matter, she wasn't coming back, anyway.

As she walked down the road, passing identical terraced houses, with their doors peeling paint and their overgrown, tiny front gardens, she pulled a mobile out of her pocket.

'Hey Alex, Stu and a mate of his are headed to Scotland, and his mate is dressed up as a copper. What the hell do you think's going on there?'

Chapter 4

Jessica hated school. What was the point? The world was fucked up anyway, with climate change. There hardly seemed any point in doing anything, especially learning about history. Who cared what happened in the 18th century when we needed to be worried about the future, about the present?

And yet here she was, in her bedroom, stuck on her computer and grappling with history homework due in tomorrow morning. Her mum would freak if she knew that Jessica had left it so late to complete her homework, but Aunt Ellie didn't have a clue about what work Jessica had or when it was due in.

Jessica stared at the mass of text displayed on her screen. It might as well have been written in Chinese, because it wouldn't have been any less illegible than it was now.

'Fuck it,' she whispered.

Jessica turned off her computer and sat on her bed. She'd had enough. She didn't care that she would get into trouble for not completing her assignment, and she didn't care if she passed or failed her exams.

Jessica gazed out of her window at the slowly darkening sky. She hated Scotland. She hated the remoteness of it all, she hated the strong, impenetrable accents that people spoke with, she hated the looks she got for being different and new. And some days she hated her mother for dragging them up here.

Jessica turned on the TV mounted on the wall and flicked through the range of shows and movies to watch. She had another twenty minutes before Aunt Ellie would call them down for dinner. Oliver was probably playing a game on his computer anyway, so Jessica should be allowed to watch something. The TV and movie choices scrolled by, turning into a blur of colour and shapes. Nothing, just nothing to watch at all.

Jessica paused browsing when she heard the knock at the front door. Weird, they never had visitors. Mum had no friends. Ollie never spoke a word to anyone and didn't go to school, so obviously he had no friends either. And Jessica never allowed her friends to visit her house. They might know her family was weird, Jessica talked about them enough, but they didn't know how weird. And Jessica wasn't about to let them find out by allowing them round to her home.

Their unexpected visitor knocked at the door again. Was Aunt Ellie going to answer it?

Jessica climbed off her bed and opened her bedroom door a little. She peered through the gap. From where she was she couldn't see the front door, only a section of the hall. She caught a glimpse of movement as Aunt Ellie hurried to answer the visitor's insistent knocks.

Jessica listened as her aunt opened the door.

'Madeline Graves?' The man's voice carried up the stairs, although it wasn't overly loud.

'No, I'm her sister Ellie.'

'Oh, I was told that Mrs Graves lived here.'

'She does, but I'm looking after her children, she's away at the moment.' Aunt Ellie paused, but the man said nothing. 'Is there something wrong?'

Another pause. 'I think it might be better if I came inside and then I can explain.'

'Yes, of course.'

What was Aunt Ellie doing, letting this man inside their house? Her eye fixed on the tiny section of the hallway that she was able to see, Jessica glimpsed a uniformed man walking by.

The police! What did the police want with her mother?

Jessica considered going downstairs. The last thing she wanted was to be dragged into a conversation with a policeman, but curiosity pulled her out of her bedroom and onto the landing. From up here the murmur of voices filtered through, but she couldn't make out what they were saying. Perhaps if she descended the stairs, got a little closer.

Crouched on the third step from the bottom, Jessica could just make out the conversation happening behind the closed door to the living room. The policeman was asking more questions about where Jessica's mother was and how long she had been away, and how could they get in touch? All the while he refused to answer any of Aunt Ellie's questions.

A worm of disquiet squirmed its way through Jessica's gut. There was something wrong here, something off about this policeman, but what it was eluded her. From the brief glimpse she'd had of him, he looked like a policeman. And there was no reason to think he wasn't.

Finally the voices fell silent. Jessica, suspecting the police officer was getting ready to leave, scooted a few steps up and out of sight of the living room door. As she settled down again, listening out for the door opening, Jessica realised what was wrong.

The policeman had a London accent. Up here, in the wilds of Scotland? How likely was that?

Jessica cocked her head. Aunt Ellie had said something. Just one word, that was all, an exclamation of surprise. This was quickly followed by a series of thin, sharp noises that Jessica had never heard before and then the thump of something heavy hitting the floor.

Jessica clutched the banister, her heart racing.

None of this sounded good. Something was wrong, but Jessica couldn't work out what.

The living room door opened.

Jessica leaned forward. Holding her hair back off her face, she could see the carpet of the hallway and the silver carpet gripper in the living room doorway. Two feet appeared, black shiny shoes and the hems of trouser legs. But that wasn't enough.

Jessica risked leaning forward some more. The man was standing in the doorway, not moving at all. She leaned forward, gripping the banister behind her to stop herself from overbalancing and tumbling down the steps. She saw more of the policeman's legs and then his waist.

At that moment he lowered his hand. He held a gun in it, a long-barrelled handgun. Was that a silencer? Was that the noise she had heard?

Jessica sat up and clamped a hand over her mouth.

Was Aunt Ellie dead?

She heard movement. The soft rustle of clothing as the man walked along the hall.

Towards the stairs.

Jessica turned and ran up the steps, not caring how much noise she made. She flew along the landing to Oliver's bedroom door and flung it open. Oliver was sitting at his desk, playing a computer game. A pair of bulky headphones covered his ears. An adjustable microphone was positioned in front of his lips, which always puzzled Jessica.

She pushed the bedroom door shut and leaned her back against it, as though that would offer protection from the threat inside her house.

'Ollie!' Jessica hissed.

The twelve-year-old continued playing.

Jessica ran up behind him and yanked the headphones from his ears. He swivelled on the chair, his face contorting into a mask of rage.

'Ollie, we need to get out of here! Aunt Ellie's dead, this man killed her and he's going to kill us next!'

Ollie's eyes widened as he looked over Jessica's shoulder. She twisted her head as the door slammed against the bedroom wall. Oliver's cricket bat, bought for his ninth birthday but left to stand neglected in the bedroom corner, hit the wooden floorboards with a loud clatter.

The policeman, or whatever he was, stood in the doorway to Ollie's bedroom, the gun held casually by his side.

'Jessica Graves?'

'Yes?' Her voice trembled, made her sound like a little girl. And why had she responded that way, like a Pavlovian dog responding to the ding of the bell?

'Oliver Graves?'

Oliver nodded.

The man raised the gun and pointed it at Jessica.

'Please, no!'

She screwed her eyes shut, waiting for the bullet. She heard a thump and opened her eyes. Amber had jumped off Oliver's cabin bed. As the cat charged out of the bedroom, the man swung the gun around and fired it. Oliver's mattress jerked as the bullet hit the foam. Strangely, there had been no sound of the gun firing, just a soft *pffffitt*. Jessica realised she had been right, the man had a silencer on the gun's barrel.

Oliver screamed. The kind that cuts through a person's head like a hot needle plunged straight into the brain.

The man winced in pain and swung around to face Oliver. 'Shut up! Shut the fuck up!'

He fired the gun again. The computer monitor exploded in a shower of plastic and fizzing sparks. Oliver tumbled off his chair and screamed again. Jessica jumped back, away from the smashed monitor which now had flames bursting from its busted insides.

But she never took her eyes off the man with the gun.

He stared wild-eyed at the two children and at the fire. The flames were licking at the curtains behind Oliver's desk. The man looked scared, panicked, as though he didn't know what to do next. This obviously wasn't how he had planned things.

Oliver stopped screaming and drew a deep breath. In that moment's relief from his screaming, they could hear the crackling and electrical fizzing of the computer on fire.

Oliver let rip with another scream, this one even more piercing than the last one. If only they had neighbours nearby, someone to notice the disturbance and call the police.

The real police.

Beads of sweat had formed on the man's forehead and his cheeks were glowing red. He was visibly stressed out by the situation, but still collected enough to point the gun at Oliver and pull the trigger.

The chamber clicked.

'Fucking hell!'

He emptied the cartridge out of the gun and it hit the floorboards at his feet. He pulled a fresh cartridge out of his pocket.

Jessica flew at him, a sudden rage filling her chest. He grunted as she smacked into his torso in a rugby tackle, barrelling him through the bedroom doorway and onto the landing. He smacked his head against the balustrade as he landed on his back on the floor, with Jessica on top of him.

'You stupid bitch!'

He grabbed a fistful of her hair and yanked her head back. She clawed at his face, trying to scratch at his eyes. He smelled of cigarettes and alcohol.

Oliver drew a breath and screamed again.

The man lifted his gun and smacked it against Jessica's head. Stars exploded in front of her and she lost control of her limbs. She tumbled to the floor and rolled onto her back.

Panting, the man clambered onto his hands and knees.

The stars receded.

The man climbed to his feet and patted at his pockets. 'Fucking hell.' He looked at the floor, searching for the cartridge he had dropped.

Jessica snapped a foot out and kicked him in the shin.

'Ow, you little bitch!'

He kicked her in the thigh and her leg went numb. He kicked her again, this time in the side. Her insides filled with an awful, sickening pain, so intense she thought she might throw up.

Tears blurred her vision and ran down her face. As the first wave of sickness slowly rolled away and gathered itself for another surge, Jessica saw the man bending down, reaching for something.

As he straightened up, he snapped the fresh cartridge into the gun.

Jessica had nothing left to fight with. This man had beaten her into submission and now all she could do was wait to die.

Strange, but her only thought left was to wonder why Oliver had stopped screaming.

The boy stepped out of his bedroom and swung his cricket bat, smashing it into the man's face. The wet crunch followed by a gurgling scream told Jessica that Oliver had put every ounce of his strength into that swing.

Jessica hauled herself up to a sitting position and wiped away the tears. The man had dropped his gun and lifted his hands to his face, which now resembled a Halloween mask. Blood poured from his mangled nose and his left cheekbone jutted out at a distressing angle. Blood leaked from his left eye, and already the eyelids were swelling shut.

'Youuckinbashtard!'

Oliver had dropped the cricket bat and stared at the man. The young boy suddenly looked horrified as he realised what he had done.

Jessica picked the bat up and swung it at the man's head. The flat side connected to his skull with a spongy crunch. The man howled and tottered back. He backed up to the top of the stairs and his feet stepped out into nothing.

Jessica flinched at the loud snap of his neck breaking as he hit the bottom.

Oliver looked at her with round, wide eyes. Realising she was still holding the cricket bat, she let it go. They both looked at the bat lying on the floor. Droplets of scarlet blood decorated the once pristine wood.

Jessica noticed there was something else on the bat, something grey and soft looking.

She turned away before she could think about it too much.

Jessica held out her hand to Oliver. He took it.

'We should go downstairs, see Aunt Ellie.' She had meant to say, *see if Aunt Ellie is alive,* but she couldn't bring herself to speak the words.

She took a couple of steps towards the stairs, but Oliver held back, tugging on her hand. Jessica looked back at him and he shook his head.

'We have to, Ollie, we can't stay here.'

Oliver shook his head again.

Jessica swallowed the urge to burst into tears. Her bottom lip started trembling. She bit down on it hard. Behind Oliver, through the doorway, Jessica could see that his curtains were ablaze now.

'Terry? What the hell's going on?'

The voice came from outside, from the front door. There were two of them then, at least.

The man pounded his fist on the door. 'Terry, what the fuck? The house is on fire! Terry?'

Jessica pulled Oliver along with her as she ran back down the landing. Their cottage was tiny and Jessica could think of nowhere to hide where they wouldn't be found in a matter of minutes. Besides which, the house was on fire. They had to get out.

Their mother's bedroom was on the left and straight ahead was the bathroom. Jessica's bedroom was on their right.

Downstairs, the front door crashed open.

Jessica dragged Oliver into her bedroom and shut the door. She ran to the window and looked out. A shiny black Range Rover sat at the top of the footpath to their cottage. The driver's door had been left open. The dashboard pinged its insistent command to close the door. The ceiling light illuminated the car's empty interior.

Just the two men, then.

Jessica scooped her mobile off her desk. Should she call the police? Her mother?

Downstairs, the man swore loudly as he discovered Terry's body.

No time to call anyone. They had to get out of the house.

Oliver opened the bedroom window and leaned out. Looked down.

'Oliver!' Maddie hissed. 'What are you doing? We can't jump out of the window!'

Oliver glanced back at Jessica's bedroom door. Gripping

the window frame, he swung one leg out and then the other. He twisted, so that he was facing back into Jessica's bedroom. Staring at Jessica, he lowered himself, disappearing from view until just his hands were left gripping the bottom frame.

He let go.

There was a thump as he hit something. Jessica leaned out of the open window and looked down.

Oliver had landed on the wheelie bin and it had toppled over. But he was fine. He was already back on his feet and lifting the wheelie bin upright again. He positioned it beneath the window.

Jessica heard the man in Oliver's bedroom next to hers.

She climbed out of the window and twisted around, just like she had seen Oliver do. She lowered herself, letting her arms straighten as she gripped the window frame. To her left, the glass in Oliver's bedroom window cracked as the flames heated it up.

The bedroom door crashed open.

Jessica closed her eyes and let go.

The drop was so brief it was over before she felt the fall. She hit the wheelie bin. She fell off it, scraping her hands on the rocky ground. Oliver grabbed her and pulled her to her feet.

Jessica risked a swift glance up to her bedroom window. Framed in the rectangle, a dark figure stared down at her, his hands on the windowsill.

Jessica and Oliver turned their backs on their house and ran.

Chapter 5

Euston Station heaved with commuters and tourists. After the last two years of living in isolation at Inverie, Maddie recoiled at the proximity of so many people. They were like cattle, being herded through gates and into pens where they waited for their trains. All those bodies, bumping up against each other, their inane chatter, their coughs and sneezes, they repulsed Maddie. Turned her stomach over with a greasy flop. She had never been totally comfortable with London's density, with the packed streets, the cars and buses, the throbbing life of the city. Jonathon had kept her here, anchored her when she craved travel and open spaces.

Maddie had given up more than her career when she married Jonathon and agreed to have children; she'd lost her freedom too. Having a family was Jonathon's idea. He had three brothers and two sisters, all married, all populating an already over-populated planet with yet more humans. Maddie resisted at first, her principles warring with a sudden maternal need for children.

Perhaps a family hadn't totally been Jonathon's idea after all, but he had been the driver, always pushing. Maddie gave birth to Jessica and then, just over two years later,

Oliver. Maddie had been ready to stop there. No more, two was perfect.

Not Jonathon. He wanted his big family, kids dashing through the house, laughing and yelling.

So they had Harry, and Maddie said no more, that's it now. Mentally she prepared herself for Jonathon's subtle attempts at persuasion, his gradual eroding of her will to resist.

Maddie wanted her freedom back. She wanted to travel again, return to her career of photography. She wanted to document the destruction of the rainforests, the coral reefs, the indigenous communities most vulnerable to the first world need for more possessions.

The children, they had held her back. The responsibility they brought with them, that was what tethered her to a city she wished she could escape. That's what she had believed. Until that day the hidden tension in the marriage erupted through the surface, and Maddie had screamed and yelled at her husband until her voice cracked and failed her.

Jonathon, he was the chain binding her. He kept her imprisoned in the city, not her children. He always promised her that one day they would leave London behind, that Maddie could have her career once more and he would follow her around the world. But not yet, not while he was building his career in the City of London, one of the world's primary financial hubs.

A family friend had opened a door for Jonathon, got him that position at Key House Accountancy. Bob Willoughby, with his expensive suits and his Jaguar, his connections in the city and beyond, and always ready with a favour for those in his inner circle.

Bob had been the one to trap Maddie in the end. If not for him, Maddie doubted Jonathon would have got that job, the cause of the argument that day.

The day Jonathon and Harry were murdered.

Euston Station's cavernous space echoed with departure announcements, thrusting Maddie back into the present. Somewhere she thought she could make out the sound of a piano being played, an odd contrast to the general hubbub of travellers passing through.

Maddie shifted the weight of her rucksack on her back.

Her mobile buzzed in her jeans pocket. Ellie, probably, calling to make sure her fragile sister was all right, and making one last attempt to persuade her to stay with her brother-in-law.

Maddie didn't recognise the number on the display. The phone vibrated in her hand, demanding to be answered. Hardly anyone knew Maddie's number, she had purposefully cut off contact with almost all family and friends after the murders. Maddie stared at the phone's screen, willing it to reveal its secrets without the need for her to answer it.

The mobile stopped vibrating, the screen reverting to the home display, a photo of the three children in happier times. About to slip the mobile back into her pocket, Maddie paused as it began buzzing again.

The need to find out more warred with her desire for privacy. Whoever it was, they seemed to be desperate to speak to her.

Curiosity won in the end.

'Hello?'

'Your children are in danger.'

A sliver of anxiety slid into her gut and twisted for good measure.

'Who is this? Why are you calling me?'

'Please, listen to me, you don't have much time, it might even be too late already.' Maddie heard movement, and something tapping. Maybe a keyboard. 'Two men have been sent to your house to murder you and your children. Call your children now, tell them to leave immediately.'

'I don't believe you,' Maddie said. 'Why are you saying these horrible things? Just who the hell do you think you are?'

'Call your daughter. Call her right now.'

Maddie disconnected the call. She couldn't bear to listen to that voice any longer. A malicious prankster, that's all they were. Tomorrow she would arrange for a new number, and then hopefully she would hear no more from this idiot.

Call your daughter. Call her right now.

That cold knife of anxiety twisted once more deep in her stomach. Yes, she should call. Not because she had been told to, but because she needed to check in with Jessica.

She pulled Jessica's number up and thumbed the call button.

It rang out until she was directed to voicemail. Maddie disconnected and tried ringing her sister instead. Again the call rang out until being transferred to voicemail.

Maddie disconnected without leaving a message. She took a deep breath and stared at her mobile, as though willing it to tell her what was going on. It was probably nothing. They were just away from their phones for the moment, that was all.

Except, Jessica's a teenager, her mobile is practically an extension of her.

Maddie decided to call the home phone. Someone would have to answer that.

But the home phone rang out too.

That cold knife of anxiety twisted again and began burning hot.

Chapter 6

Jessica glanced back over her shoulder. The man at the window was no longer there.

'Keep running!' she hissed.

Oliver was panting and stumbling. He'd never been a physically active child, even when he had been at school and had to go to PE lessons. It wasn't going to be long before he would tire and slow to a halt. Unless, of course, the adrenaline rush of fleeing a man intent on killing him kept him going.

A light rain had started falling, the raindrops so tiny they almost formed a mist. The heavy clouds in the evening sky indicated there was heavier rain to come. The last golden rays of sunlight, sneaking through a gap in the cloud on the horizon, illuminated the footpath just enough for them to navigate their way. Soon though, the sun would have set and they would be plunged into darkness without even the moon and stars for light.

The children stumbled up the path and past the Range Rover, which was still making pinging noises. Jessica fleetingly wondered if the keys were still in the ignition, and maybe they could drive out of here. But she had never had a driving lesson, and the path out of their bay was rocky enough that only experienced drivers could attempt it.

They had a better chance on foot.

Jessica grabbed Oliver by the wrist and dragged him up the rocky path. To their right, a steep drop to the sea. To their left a steep rise into woods. The rocky trail led up to a tarmac road, which would take them to the small harbour where Jessica was taken by boat to the mainland every school morning. But they didn't live on an island, and the road curved around the bay and finally took them to the mainland. The boat was faster, that was all.

If they stayed on the path, then their pursuer would catch up with them, but if they escaped into the forest, they had a chance. They could get to the harbour, and just hope that the harbour master was still there.

Jessica spotted what she had been looking out for; a frayed rope hanging from a branch. With knots along its length, it was ideal for swinging and climbing.

'Quick, climb the rope, into the forest!' Jessica hissed.

Oliver stopped and looked at her. The slam shut of a car door carried through the evening to them.

Jessica pushed Oliver at the rope. 'Use your hands to climb the rope and your feet on the bank. I'll help you.'

The Range Rover's engine rumbled into life.

Oliver grabbed the rope and hauled himself up, his feet scrabbling at the soil bank. Jessica's chest tightened with dismay as she realised Oliver had only a pair of socks on his feet. Her situation was barely any better as she was wearing slippers.

Jessica bent down and planted her hands on his skinny bottom and pushed. With her help, Oliver managed to climb the rope. He snatched at a root protruding from the bank of earth, Jessica still shoving him up and in to the packed wall of dark soil.

Twin beams of light cut through the evening gloom, like searchlights probing the darkness for their quarry. The beams jerked crazily from side to side as the Range Rover tackled the rocky trail. The vehicle wasn't visible yet, still below a ridge on the trail, but Jessica could see by the headlight beams that it was drawing closer.

'Get a move on!' Jessica gave Oliver a hard shove into the packed bank of earth, and he managed to scramble up and onto the edge.

The note of the Range Rover's engine changed as it took a steep section of the trail. Jessica heard tyres scrabbling against pebbles before they got traction. She hauled herself up the knotted rope much faster than Oliver. Before she reached out for the thick root, Jessica glanced back.

The Range Rover appeared into view and Jessica squinted as the headlights swept over her. She reached out and closed her fist around the root and pulled herself in to the bank of earth. With two quick moves, she was up and on to the edge. On all fours, she scrambled into the forest, her hands and knees snapping twigs like firecrackers.

They had to move fast. The man had to have seen Jessica, frozen like a rabbit in the headlights of an oncoming car. He would follow them into the forest.

And if he found them, he would kill them.

'Ollie!' Jessica remained on all fours, motionless, searching for Oliver. The headlights had dazzled her, and their ghostly image hovered over the darkness of the forest, obscuring her sight. She couldn't even try to listen for Oliver, the noise of the Range Rover fighting its way up the rocky trail filled the evening.

Jessica heard the ratchet of a handbrake being pulled on and then the engine died. The sudden silence assaulted Jessica's ears. It didn't last long. The sound of the car door opening and then slamming shut carried through the night.

Where was Oliver? Had he escaped into the forest without Jessica?

A grunt, followed by the rustling of leaves behind Jessica, cut through the night. The man was climbing the rope.

Wherever Oliver was, Jessica couldn't wait for him any longer. She had to get out of here.

Just as she was about to climb to her feet, Jessica spotted movement in the darkness and flinched as a hand grabbed her arm.

Oliver, just visible in the gloom. His face streaked with dirt, eyes wide with fear.

Holding on to each other, they scrambled deeper into the forest. They had to move slowly as they could barely see anything in the darkness. The last of the sun's dying rays of golden light had disappeared. Although they had to move slowly and carefully between the trees hidden in the dark, Jessica realised they had an advantage over their pursuer; Oliver spent much of his time alone in the woods, and he was familiar with it.

The man chasing them was in alien territory and he was effectively blind.

A sharp crack and a cry of pain in the darkness confirmed Jessica's thoughts.

Jessica pulled Oliver to a halt. 'We need to get down to the harbour. Can you find your way?'

Oliver, just visible to Jessica in the deep gloom, nodded. He grabbed her hand and guided her with him, their faces lowered as twigs and branches scraped at their heads and shoulders.

Another cry of pain cut through the forest.

'You little shits! I'm going to shoot you both in the fucking head when I find you!'

Oliver stopped, frozen in place. His grip on Jessica's hand grew tighter, squeezing her fingers together.

'We've got to keep moving,' Jessica whispered. 'He can't keep up with us, not in here, but we have to go before he finds us.'

Oliver's grip on Jessica's hand lessened a little, and he pulled her forward once more. With her free hand, Jessica reached out to steady herself. Her trembling fingers found branches and leaves, the rough texture of bark and soft mounds of moss.

They crept through the darkness, their feet snagging in the undergrowth. Jessica's slippers were soaked. Every root and twig she stepped on poked its way through the thin sole and into the soft flesh of her foot.

Something scurried across her foot, and Jessica yelped. Turning and glaring at her, Oliver placed a finger against his lips.

'Wait!' Jessica hissed.

Motionless, they stood and listened. Jessica heard the waves lapping gently at the shore of Loch Nevis. A creature scuffling through the undergrowth. The soft murmuration of the leaves in a gentle breeze.

But there were no sounds of snapping twigs and cries of pain or frustration.

'I think he's given up.' Jessica stared at her brother, desperate for him to agree and to make her statement come true.

He shook his head and pointed ahead of them.

'All right, let's go.'

They stumbled through the dense woodland, Oliver leading the way. The trees opened out and Jessica saw the sea, the dark bulk of Ladhar Bheinn in the distance just visible against the sky.

Most of all she saw the boat, tethered to the harbour and bobbing up and down in the gentle swell. The boat was powered by an outboard motor. Jessica knew they couldn't use that, but there were oars in the boat in case the motor broke down.

Both the children were crouching just inside the edge of the woodland. The rocky track leading down to the cottage separated them from the footpath to the harbour.

'We're almost there, Ollie,' Jessica whispered. 'We'll take the boat over to the mainland and get help.'

Jessica climbed to her feet and froze.

The Range Rover's engine rumbled into life, its deep growl carrying in the night like a warning to trespassers into its domain. Jessica and Oliver shrank back into the shadows of the forest. Gears crunching and tyres skidding on the rocks, the vehicle drew closer. The twin beams of its headlights appeared first, cutting through the darkness. The Range Rover bounced and rocked on its suspension as it rounded a bend.

The vehicle drew closer. Oliver's grip on Jessica's hand began tightening painfully. It drove past them, close enough that Jessica saw the driver twisting his head from side to side as he searched for the children.

He drove past, his quarry cloaked by the darkness of the forest.

Jessica waited until the Range Rover had disappeared from view around another bend in the track.

'Come on, before he comes back!' Jessica yanked Oliver's hand and they dropped from the wooded bank down onto the trail. Oliver sucked in a sharp breath as his bare feet hit the ground.

They stumbled down the footpath to the boat and climbed in. Its sides bumped against the tiny jetty with their movements. Jessica checked the oars were in their usual place. She turned her attention to the rope tied to the post. Her numb, trembling fingers clawed at the knot. Jessica cried out in frustration.

Oliver prodded urgently at her shoulder.

Rounding on him, Jessica hissed, 'What?'

Then she saw it, the Range Rover's headlights heading back towards them. The driver had turned around at the top of the track where it met the road and begun heading back.

'Lie down!'

There was nothing in the boat apart from the oars. No tarpaulin to hide under. They were in plain sight. Unless they lay down in the bottom of the boat. It was their only hope.

Jessica pulled Oliver down with her and they wriggled themselves under the two benches. Brackish water soaked through their clothes and Jessica wrinkled her nose at the smell. She jammed herself into the boat's hull, trying to make herself as small as possible. Oliver copied Jessica on the opposite side.

The Range Rover pulled to a stop by the harbour. The engine idled.

Had he seen them?

Jessica heard the door opening and slamming shut. Still the engine continued running.

Footsteps on the wooden jetty, drawing closer.

'The Graves woman, she's not here, she's in fuckin' London according to her sister.'

The hollow thud of footsteps drew closer and then paused.

'She's dead, but the kids ran away. Fuck knows where they are now.'

Jessica held her breath.

'Nah, Terry's dead, the little shits fucked him over with a cricket bat.'

The boat creaked as it lifted and dropped in the gentle swell.

'No shit the operation's gone south, don't you think I already know that? I'm right here, stuck in the middle of this crap.'

Jessica's head tingled with the effort of holding her breath. She let her breath go, slowly, silently and breathed in.

'Ah, for fuck's sake Mac, are you fucking serious? It's the arse end of nowhere out here, how the fuck do you expect me to find them?'

Please, just go. Leave, give up now and leave.

'All right, all right, don't blow a fuckin' gasket, I'll speak to you later.'

Feet shifting on the dock, the rustle of clothing followed

by the strike and flare of a match. Jessica heard a deep sigh and then smelled tobacco smoke.

'Fuck's sake, where are you, you little brats?'

He shifted position on the dock again, the soles of his boots scraping against the wood.

Silence.

A metallic click.

'All right, I can see you. Come on out.'

Jessica stiffened. She was hiding in the side of the boat next to the dock. The man had to have spotted Oliver, but Jessica couldn't be certain because she had her back to him.

'Look, you little brat, don't make me come down there and drag you out. I'm not going to hurt you, all right?'

Silence. No sounds of movement from Oliver.

'Is your sister hiding in there too? Both of you, get out of the fucking boat now.'

Still no movement from Oliver, and Jessica's limbs felt frozen in place.

'Fuck's sake.'

A gunshot tore the night apart. Jessica screamed and twisted onto her back, expecting to see Oliver dead, his skull smashed open and leaking brains over the boat's hull.

He was uninjured.

Unlike the boat, which now had a large hole in its hull and was rapidly filling up with water.

Oliver scrambled out from his hiding place and onto the jetty. Jessica followed him, the cold water soaking through her slippers. Sitting on the hard deck of the jetty next to her brother, she looked up at the man. He was a shadow in the darkness, his mouth and the tip of his nose revealed for a moment in the orange glow from his cigarette tip.

'Yeah, I thought that would get you moving.' He waved the gun at them and pointed it at the Range Rover. 'Get in the car, we're going on a little trip to the Big Smoke. You're not going to see the Queen's jewels or anything though.'

Jessica's breath hitched as she attempted to speak. The last thing she wanted was to burst into tears in front of this man. But she had to try to talk, to find out why he was doing this.

'Why... why are—?'

'Just shut the fuck up, all right? I'm not here to babysit you or nothing, I'm your taxi driver, that's all. Get in the car, keep your traps shut, and don't give me any bother. That way I might let you live.'

Behind Jessica, the boat gurgled as it sank into the cold water of Loch Nevin.

The man waved his gun at them again. 'All right, chop-chop you little toe-rags! We've got a very long and extremely fuckin' boring drive ahead of us.'

Jessica climbed slowly to her feet along with her brother. She slipped the slippers swollen with water off her feet.

The man flicked his cigarette away, bright sparks flying as it dropped to the water.

Jessica and Oliver trod gingerly up the path to the Range Rover and climbed into the back seats.

Looking out of the window, Jessica saw the man talking on his phone.

She closed her eyes.

It seemed pointless to question why they were being taken back to London. Once they got there, Jessica was sure of only one thing.

They were going to die.

Chapter 7

What to do? What to do?

With no one answering the phone at the cottage in Scotland, Maddie had no idea who to try next.

The police, maybe? But that seemed ridiculous. If not for the crank call about her children being in danger, Maddie would have no concerns about their safety. She would have been on her way to the Premier Inn where she was staying the night.

Had it been a crank call?

Maddie had no way of knowing until she spoke to her children or her sister. The thought of calling the police seemed ridiculous. What would she do, call 999? Was this classed as an emergency? Perhaps she should call a local police station near Inverie. They could send someone over to check on Ellie and the children.

Maddie Googled the nearest police station to Inverie. *Edinburgh.* Seriously? That was the closest?

Maddie tapped the number on the screen and put the phone to her ear. She placed her free hand over her other ear. The noise from that tannoy seemed to be growing louder.

The number rang out until finally there was a click.

'Hello, I—'

'Thank you for contacting the Edinburgh Police. All of our operatives are dealing with other calls at the moment, but your call is important to us and the next available operative will be with you soon. If your call is an emergency, please hang up and dial 999. If your call is not an emergency and you need to report a crime for insurance purposes, it may be quicker for you to visit our website and use the chat function. Visit us on—'

Maddie hung up.

Why did everything have to be automated?

Maddie dialled her sister's number again.

Come on, Ellie, answer the phone. Answer the phone.

When she got to voicemail, Maddie almost hung up, but stopped herself. 'Hey, Ellie, just letting you know I'm in London now. Look, I've had a weird phonecall, and it's probably nothing, but could you call me back as soon as you get this message? Bye.'

Maddie hung up.

A crowd of commuters surged around her, disgorged from a recently arrived train. Maddie was jostled and knocked as they rushed for the exit. She took a deep breath, pushed the urge to yell and lash out at the commuters surrounding her deep down inside. She had to stay in control.

The mobile burst into life. Barely glancing at the screen, Maddie answered it.

'Ellie? Thanks for calling ba—'

'Did you speak to them? Your children, did you get them out of the house?'

The inside of Maddie's mouth dried up. She swallowed and her throat clicked.

'No. They aren't answering their phones.'
Silence.
'Who is this? Are you the police?'
'Don't call the police, they can't help you.'
'But who—?'
'No more questions. It's best if we meet. Stay where you are, someone will collect you.'
'But how do you know where I am?'
The disconnected tone hummed in Maddie's ear.
'Oh no you don't,' she muttered. 'I need answers.'
Maddie thumbed the return call button. Instead of a ring tone she got an automated message.

The number you have called is not in use.

Maddie listened as the short, simple message was repeated again and again. Finally she hung up.

What now? Just wait here until this mystery person came and collected her? And then what? Allow them to take her somewhere they could murder her? And all the time having no idea what danger, if any, her children were in?

The number you have called is not in use.
Don't call the police, they can't help you.

'Bollocks,' Maddie whispered.

She couldn't just stand here waiting for someone who might or might not turn up, whilst her children might or might not be in danger. And even if this mystery caller did turn up, how could Maddie know what their intentions were? Why would they tell her to not call the police if they had good intentions? None of it made any sense.

No, it was time to call the police. And this time Maddie was dialing 999. As far as she was concerned, this was most definitely an emergency.

Before she could tap in the number, Maddie's mobile burst into life once more, buzzing in her hand.

Please let it be Ellie, she thought. But the number was not one she knew.

Her mystery caller again?

'Hello?'

'Mrs Graves, we have your children.'

Maddie sucked in a sharp breath. This was a new voice, one filled with menace. 'Where are they? What's happened to them?'

'They're safe and unharmed, but we are keeping hold of them for the moment.'

'What do you mean you're keeping hold of them? Let me speak to Jessica.'

'You can speak to them later, but right now—'

'Shut up!' Maddie lowered her voice and bowed her head. 'Just shut up and let me talk. Put Jessica on the phone right now or I am calling the police.'

'I would advise against that, Mrs Graves. Once you call the police, you will have lost any possibility of seeing your children alive again.'

Don't call the police, they can't help you.

Maddie squeezed her eyes shut. Tears gathered around her lashes.

The number you have called is not in use.

'Mrs Graves, listen to me. If you follow my instructions, you will be reunited with Jessica and Oliver very soon. Do you understand?'

Ellie. This man, whoever he was, had not mentioned Ellie. What did that mean? Was she dead?

'Mrs Graves, do you understand what I am telling you?'

Maddie worked some saliva into her mouth and swallowed. 'Yes, I understand.'

'Good. First of all, let me repeat, you must not call the police. They cannot help you. Please tell me you understand.'

Did he realise he was the second person to tell her this? Were these two men connected somehow? But that didn't make sense, as one had tried to warn her of the danger to Jessica and Oliver, and the other one claimed to have kidnapped them.

'Mrs Graves!'

His voice was sharp, growing impatient.

'Yes, I understand, no police.'

What was that noise in the background? There was something familiar about it, even though it was little more than an indistinct rumble.

'Good. Now, I have an address for you. Make a note of it. You are to come straight here. Don't talk to anyone, don't phone anyone, don't text anyone, don't post on your Facebook profile, absolutely nothing, okay?'

Maddie nodded. That noise, she thought she recognised it now. Was this man speaking to her from a car?

'Mrs Graves, did you hear me?'

'Yes, I heard you.'

'Good. Make a note of this address. 128 Bolingbroke Road, West Southern Way. Have you got that?'

'Yes.'

The man hung up, the phone line dead.

Maddie's mobile phone slipped from her fingers. Through a sudden haze of grey, she heard the crack of the casing as it hit the station floor. Before she was fully aware of what was happening, her knees buckled. Someone gasped. Hands grabbed at her, fingers catching at her clothes and then falling away.

Maddie's body seemed to fold in on itself and she crumpled to the floor, as though her bones had suddenly left her body to hold itself up. The weight of the rucksack carried her backwards, but cushioned her fall. She rolled over onto her side, her left arm twisted beneath her torso and her right arm flung behind her. Voices floated in and out of her hearing.

Did you see that?
She just fainted!
Is she having a fit?
Someone call an ambulance!

'No,' Maddie muttered. 'No ambulance.'

Hands lifted her, pulling the rucksack off her back and laying her head on something soft laid on the floor as a makeshift pillow. A face hovered into view as the grey haze receded.

'What did you say?'

'No ambulance.'

The face turned and looked up at the crowd of other faces peering down at Maddie. 'She says she doesn't want an ambulance.'

Maddie straightened herself out and pushed her elbows against the hard floor. As she sat up, the floor began to spin and wobble. Maddie lay back down again.

The face turned back to her. A middle-aged man, round glasses like John Lennon used to wear, his eyes wide with concern.

'Lie still for a minute, you fainted.'

'I know.' Maddie blinked, her vision clear once more, the strength returning to her limbs. 'I'm all right, I just need a moment.'

'Should we call for an ambulance?'

'No, I'm fine, thank you.'

Maddie placed her palms flat against the cold station floor. Tested it out, checking if it was still pretending to be a seesaw. She pushed herself up, bracing for a sudden tilting.

Her world remained steady.

'Here, you dropped this.' John Lennon held out her mobile, a spider's web of cracks decorating the screen. 'It might still work.'

Maddie took it and pressed the power button. The screen lit up.

She pocketed the phone and climbed unsteadily to her feet. Hands stretched out to help her, but hovered inches away, reluctant to invade her personal space now that she was conscious and standing.

'There's a bench over there, you should sit down for a moment,' John Lennon said.

Maddie nodded. He picked up her rucksack and walked with her to the bench. Maddie sat down and the man placed her rucksack on the bench next to her.

'Is there anything else I can do to help?'

'No.' Maddie shook her head. The crowd had dispersed. He was the only one left.

'Okay, if you're sure.' He hovered, unsure if he should leave or stay.

'I'm fine.' Maddie looked up at him. 'Thank you.'

'Okay, if you're sure. Look after yourself.' He gave her a faint smile and walked away.

Maddie flinched at the sudden, discordant sound of piano keys being bashed. Next to the bench, an upright piano was being attacked by a little boy. Kneeling on the stool, he pounded at the keys with the flat of his hands, fingers splayed out, his face screwed up in determination. His mother stood nearby, a look of pride on her face.

Maddie stood up. She hoisted the rucksack onto her back. Her strength had returned.

It was time to go.

Chapter 8

An anonymous, rundown town. Endless streets lined with houses, some boarded up, many still lived in but looking unfit for habitation. Maddie walked fast, almost running, following the instructions given to her over the phone. A Burqa wearing woman pushed a buggy with a listless child sitting in it. A flatbed truck drove past, four tattooed white men sitting in the back. They shouted abuse at the woman and the driver sounded his horn.

A street lamp flickered into life as darkness slowly closed in. This place looked threatening enough in daylight, but now as night drew in and the shadows lengthened Maddie's uneasiness grew like a tumour in her stomach.

Maddie put her head down and kept walking. An old man shuffled past, muttering under his breath. Straggles of his wispy hair clung to his scalp.

The evening air wrapped around Maddie's skin like a hot towel. The humidity levels had to be off the scale.

Maddie arrived at the address she had been given. The walk had taken her up and down streets and she was sure she had been switching back on herself. All this time she had probably been under surveillance to make sure she was alone.

The house was an end terrace. The house next to it looked empty, although Maddie guessed it could be occupied with squatters. She entered the tiny garden and knocked on the door, just as she had been instructed.

The door opened immediately. The man wore a vest and loose-fitting trousers. His head was shaved, but a vast tangle of beard covered his chin and neck and lay against his huge belly. He scowled at Maddie and jerked his thumb back into the darkened hallway.

Maddie stepped inside. She had to squeeze past his bulk in the narrow hallway and he made no effort to move out of the way. She caught a whiff of stale sweat as he shut the door and locked it.

'In there.' He pointed to an open door.

Maddie stepped through and into the tiny living room. Two settees with sheets thrown over them sat at right angles to each other. A man and a woman sat on one settee and the other was empty. They were crowded around a coffee table. The room was thick with smoke. A deck of cards sat on the table, and a glass ashtray overflowing with cigarette butts. In another corner sat an old woman in a broken down wingback chair, toothlessly chewing on something. The man, wearing just a pair of ratty jeans, was playing a computer game with the skinny girl sat next to him. The harsh, staccato bursts of gunfire filled the room, along with the wet splat of bodies being ripped apart.

The vest wearing man held out a calloused hand. 'Give me your phone.'

Maddie hesitated. 'Where are my children?'

'You'll see them in a minute, now give me your phone.'

Maddie placed the mobile in the man's hand. His fist

closed around it and he slipped it in a pocket.

'Sit down.'

Maddie took a step towards the vacant settee.

'Not there.'

Maddie paused, took a look around the tiny room. There were no other seats.

'Sit on the floor, here.' The man pointed to a spot on the filthy, threadbare carpet by the wall.

Maddie got down on the floor and sat with her back against the wall. 'Where are my children?'

The man sat on the settee and picked up the deck of cards. 'You'll see them soon enough.'

'I want to see them now.'

'You need to shut that mouth of yours, or else you won't get to see them at all.'

'I was promised, the man I spoke to on the phone, is he here? He promised me I would see my children.'

'Fuck's sake, lady, don't you listen?' The man pulled a gun out from behind him and placed it on the table. He had to have had it stuffed in his trouser waistband. The man went back to studying his cards. The gun lay on the table, the muzzle pointed at Maddie.

A car drove by outside. A heavy drop of rain splatted against the living room window. The man sitting on the other settee, his bare torso covered in ugly tattoos, looked at the window.

'Looks like it's going to piss it down, Wayne.' The cigarette clamped between his lips bobbed up and down as he talked.

The man in the vest, Wayne presumably, grunted.

Maddie wrapped her arms around her torso and

jammed her hands beneath her arms to hide the shaking. Wayne didn't seem concerned that his name had been revealed. Did that mean they had no intention of letting Maddie leave here alive?

If so, what did she have to lose?

'My children, I want to see them now.'

Wayne tipped his head back and groaned. 'Fuck's sake, I knew this was a fucking mistake.'

'Let me see my children right now, or I start screaming.'

The girl on the sofa, eyes fixed on the TV screen and her thumbs flying over the game controller, snorted with derision. 'Scream all you want, nobody's going to hear you.'

Maddie threw her head back, took a deep lungful of air, and let loose with an Oliver special.

Wayne snatched his gun off the table and pointed it in Maddie's face. 'Shut the fuck up!'

Maddie stopped screaming.

She tried to not focus on the gun, did her best to meet Wayne's eyes instead. To hold his stare.

'Let me see my children, or I will scream again.'

'If you do, I will shoot you right between the eyes.'

Maddie filled her lungs with air and let rip again, screaming right in Wayne's face.

The back-handed slap knocked her to the floor. Her cheek scraped against the threadbare carpet and she lay there for a moment, too stunned to move. A tiny spider scurried away and beneath a gap in the skirting board.

The stinging pain bloomed on her cheek where she had been hit.

'Stop with all the screaming.' Wayne towered over her

and pointed to a corner of the room. 'See my mother over there?'

Maddie shifted her head to look. The old woman grinned back at her, exposing two rows of red raw gums. She was still chewing and Maddie caught a glimpse of something inside her mouth, grey and glistening. A thin line of spittle ran down her chin.

'Well she doesn't like lots of noise, it upsets her.' Wayne leaned in closer, seemed like he was blotting out all the light. 'And fuck me, but when she gets upset we all fucking know about it. So you need to keep your trap shut, all right?' He held the gun in her face. 'Because if you don't I'll take you out the back and put a bullet in your head, and then you'll never see your kids.'

White hot anger burned in Maddie's chest. Her instinct was to spit in his face and scream again. What was wrong with her? She needed to do as he commanded her.

'Do you understand me?' Wayne tapped the muzzle of the gun against her temple. 'Hello? Is there anybody in there?'

Maddie worked some saliva into her dry mouth. 'If you were going to kill me, you would have done it by now.'

'Dean, did you hear that?' Wayne straightened up and turned to Dean. 'She says I won't shoot her because I would have done it already if I could.'

'Aren't you supposed to keep her alive?' the girl said.

'Shut the fuck up, Janis. Did I ask for your stupid fucking opinion? Was I talking to you? Is your name Dean all of a fucking sudden?'

'I was just saying.'

'Well don't, you stupid cow. Don't say anything. Keep

it fucking zipped, all right?'

'Fuck off, Wayne.'

'What did you say?'

'You heard me.'

'Say it again.'

'Fuck off, Wayne.'

Maddie lay still, waiting for Wayne to lose his temper and start pulling the trigger on that gun. And once Wayne started shooting, Maddie had the awful feeling that he wouldn't stop until everybody in the room was dead.

'What's all this shouting about?'

Maddie closed her eyes. How many people were there in this nightmare of a house? This one sounded like an older man.

'Wayne, put that gun away.'

'Aww, Dad, it's Janis, she's fucking doing my head in.'

'Put the gun away.'

Maddie heard Wayne huffing and muttering, but not making any further protests. She opened her eyes as she sensed someone approaching her.

'Now come on you, sit up.' Hands mottled with freckles and lined with veins gripped Maddie's arm and helped her up. The old man was surprisingly strong. 'Do you want to sit on the settee? Dean and Janis can squish up and make room for you.'

Maddie shook her head. Her cheek throbbed and tears had gathered in her eyelashes. Wayne had sat down and picked up the deck of cards. He began laying them out on the coffee table for a game of Patience. Dean and Janis were back in their game of shooting zombies.

'What's keeping them, do you think?' Wayne said.

The old man glanced out of the rain-spattered window. 'They've got a long way to go yet, I reckon they only set off a couple of hours ago.'

Wayne glanced at Maddie. 'Fucking great.'

Dean yelped as his game's avatar fell before a horde of grunting, moaning zombies. His half of the TV screen turned red and then black.

Maddie had jerked awake at the sound of Dean shouting. The tiny room had filled with the stench of stale cigarette smoke and bodies. Maddie's back and neck ached and her bottom was sore from sitting on the floor for so long. What time was it? How many hours had she sat here, waiting for her children to be delivered to her? It had to be the middle of the night by now.

'Ah, fuck it.' Dean tossed the game controller to the floor and pulled a squashed packet of cigarettes out of his back pocket. He held the pack out. 'Anyone for a ciggie?'

'Yeah, I'll have one,' Wayne said. He'd long since lost interest in playing Patience, the cards now scattered across the coffee table.

'Me too. Janis, why don't you make us all a cup of tea?' the father said, and sat down next to Wayne. 'Mother! Would you like a cup of tea?'

Mother grinned and nodded and chewed.

'Go on Janis, a cup of tea for everyone.'

'I'm playing,' Janis said, eyes on the TV and thumbs furiously pushing buttons on the controller.

Dean snatched it off her and threw it across the room. 'Not now you're not!'

'Dean!' Janis threw herself at her brother, clawed hands going straight for his face. Dean fell on his back on the settee, laughing.

Wayne heaved his bulk off the sofa and hitched his trousers up.

'Don't leave me here on my own!' Dean yelled.

Janis paused her attack. 'Yeah, where are you going?'

'For a shit, you want to come with me? You could wipe my arse.' Wayne pulled the gun out of his waistband and placed it on the table.

Dean snickered.

'Mind your language now,' Mac said, glancing at Maddie. 'We've got a lady in the house.'

Wayne pulled a folded up newspaper from his back pocket, giving Janis a look that dared her to make a comment. He ambled out of the living room. Maddie heard the click of a lock from the hall.

'Fuck's sake, he'll be hours in there,' Janis said. 'Didn't he have a shit earlier?'

'Nah, the payload's still waiting to be released.' Dean snickered again.

Janis stood up. 'All right, I'm putting the kettle on, who wants a drink?'

'Yeah, I'll have a tea,' Dean said.

Mac nodded. 'Same here, and don't forget your mother.'

Janis glanced at Maddie and then left the room without saying anything.

Maddie heard a car pulling up outside the house.

Dean stood up and peered out of the rain splattered window. 'They're here.'

He left the room and Maddie listened to the sound of the front door opening. The hiss of rain hitting the ground grew louder.

'What the fuck kept you so long, Stu?'

Maddie heard car doors opening and shutting.

'Fuck off, Dean.'

Maddie kept her head down and stared at the grubby, threadbare carpet. She had tried acting up and demanding to see Jessica and Oliver, and that had ended badly. Right now, she needed to stay as quiet as possible.

More movement outside as people entered the house.

'It's fucking pissing it down out there.'

'No shit, Sherlock.'

'These two cause you any trouble?'

'Besides killing Terry, you mean? Little bastards.'

'Yeah, well, they'll pay for that soon enough.'

Maddie's head snapped up. Mac gave her a look, a 'hold your shit together and keep quiet' look.

Maddie bit her bottom lip and screwed her eyes shut. It had to be Jessica and Oliver. It had to be.

'Send them in here,' Mac called out.

Maddie opened her eyes and twisted her head around.

Jessica appeared in the doorway with Oliver behind her. Jessica looked close to tears but she was holding it together.

Dean shoved them both in their backs. 'In you go.'

The children ran to Maddie and threw their arms around her. Maddie hugged them, fighting back her tears.

Maddie heard the front door being shut. Dean walked back into the living room, followed by Stu.

The rain drummed at the window.

'It's fucking nasty out there.' Dean sank into the sofa and eyed Maddie and her children. 'How long have we got to babysit these three for?'

'As long as it takes,' Stu said. 'The boss wants a word with them first. Wants to find out what they know, who they've told, that kind of thing.' Stu looked at the open living room door. 'Where's Wayne?'

'Where do you think? He's back in the shitter.'

Stu raised an eyebrow. 'Seriously? He was in there when I left. Fuck me.'

Janis entered the room with four mugs of tea in her hands. She ignored Maddie and her children.

Maddie held Jessica and Oliver close, one on either side, and willed Oliver to stay calm. If he started acting up and screaming, she didn't like to think what might happen. Although her instincts told her that Mac was in charge, she wondered how much power he actually held over his family.

Dean took his mug of tea from Janis. 'Did you put four sugars in it?'

Janis tossed her head back, flicking strands of greasy hair off her face. 'You never said you wanted four sugars.'

'I always have four sugars in my tea. How many did you put in?'

'Two, like you always have.'

'Nah, I have four now. Four heaped spoons, yeah?'

'Since when did you have four sugars in your tea?'

'Fuck knows, Janis, what is this, a fucking interrogation?'

'The point is, Dean, how the fuck am I expected to

know you want four sugars in your fucking tea?'

Dean looked at his mug of tea. 'I didn't ask for milk, did I? But you still put milk in there.'

Janis rolled her eyes. 'Fuck's sake, you always have milk in your tea.'

Dean lifted his gaze to Janis once more. 'I might not, I might have changed my mind.'

'All right, all right, give me the fucking mug back.'

Janis snatched the mug of tea from Dean, spilling some on the coffee table. She turned to face Mac.

'What about you?'

Mac raised a hand. 'No, mine looks lovely Janis.' The cigarette bobbed up and down between his lips as he spoke. 'Here, hand me Mother's drink, I'll give it to her. Now, you cooled it down with cold water, didn't you?'

'Of course I did.' Janis turned to Stu. 'I suppose you want a drink now.'

Stu grinned. 'Aww, my little sister, aren't you lovely? Yeah, as it comes Janis, I'm not fussed.'

'Four sugars, yeah?' Dean said. 'And heaped spoonfuls, all right?'

Janis left the living room.

Dean looked at Oliver. 'What the fuck are you staring at, weirdo?'

Oliver stared back at Dean, wide-eyed and mute.

'Don't bother, the kid doesn't say a word, not a peep.'

'Yeah? Seriously?' Dean shifted on the settee, sitting upright and leaning towards Oliver. 'C'mon kid, say something, anything.'

Dean and Stu stared at Oliver, waiting.

Maddie's voice broke the silence, shocking even her. 'He

can't speak.'

'The fuck?' Dean grinned, obviously not quite believing what he was hearing. 'What, like he never learnt how or something?'

Maddie wished she hadn't said anything. Now she was going to have to answer Dean's questions. 'Yes, he learnt how to talk, but now... he can't.'

'Yeah? Was he, like, in an accident or something?'

'No.' Maddie thought for a second about how much she wanted to reveal of Oliver's condition. 'He just, he just kind of decided one day he wasn't going to say anything anymore. It's quite common, it's called being an elective mute.'

Dean settled back on the settee once more. 'Fucking weirdo.'

Janis entered the living room again, Dean's mug of tea clutched in one hand and Stu's in the other.

'Thanks, Sis,' Stu said, taking his mug.

'There, happy now?'

Dean took his mug of tea and looked at it. 'What the fuck? Where's the fucking milk?'

Janis threw her hands in the air in a gesture that might have been funny but for the circumstances and the tension. 'Are you fucking kidding me? You fucking said you didn't want any fucking milk in your fucking tea!'

'Nah, Janis, that's not what I said at all.' Dean held the mug out. 'I said, I might change my mind and not have milk one day, but I didn't say I had changed my fucking mind. Fuck's sake, it's not that fucking complicated. All I want is a fucking cup of tea, with milk, and four fucking sugars in it. All right?'

Janis snatched the mug of tea out of Dean's hand and hurled it across the room where it shattered against the fireplace.

'Fuck you, you little shit. You can make your own cup of tea.'

Dean stood up and bared his teeth.

'Ladies, calm down.' Stu had remained seated, but he looked ready to jump to his feet if needed. 'Put your handbags away, both of you.'

Neither of them backed away. Maddie could see cords of muscle tensing in Janis's skinny arms, and the tendons standing out in her neck. If these two had a fight, Maddie had to get the children out. There was no room in here for those two to batter each other without hurting anybody else in the vicinity.

Outside, in the hall, there was the click of a lock and the sound of a door being opened.

'Ahh, we've got a problem out here,' Wayne called from the hall.

'And I've got two fucking problems in here,' Mac shouted. 'What's wrong?'

'The crapper's blocked up.'

Janis and Dean burst into giggles and the tension evaporated.

'Aww, come on, it's not my fault!'

Dean fell back onto the settee, laughing helplessly. Janis doubled up, hands on her knees, crying with laughter.

Stu shook his head. 'I don't fucking believe it.'

Mac turned away from his wife, her cup of tea in his hand. 'Wayne, you're just going to have to sort it out yourself. Use the plunger.'

Wayne appeared in the doorway. His face was bright red and dotted with drops of sweat. Dean saw him, pointed, and burst into howls of laughter.

'Shut up, Dean,' Wayne said.

'You must be very proud,' Dean gasped. 'What are you going to call it?'

Janis collapsed on the settee and clutched her stomach, her laugh like a donkey's bray.

Wayne glowered at them both. 'Very funny.'

'All right you two, knock it off,' Mac said, chuckling.

Wayne shifted from foot to foot. 'Dad, there's another problem.'

'What?'

Wayne wiped a forearm across his sweat covered brow. 'The fucking cistern on the toilet is broken. The water's overflowing the toilet bowl.'

'Oh, bloody hell.' Mac gripped the edge of the sofa and braced himself against it as he climbed to his feet. 'Stu, go and have a look, see what he's talking about.'

Stu got up and ambled past Wayne out of the living room.

Janis and Dean continued laughing. Janis had tears running down her face.

'Fucking hell!' Stu yelled.

The squelching of the wet carpet in the hall preceded Stu returning to the living room. 'Right, you three go find the stopcock and turn the water off. We've got fucking shitty water flooding everywhere.'

Janis and Dean quit laughing and stood up. Maddie followed their stares and saw water seeping through the carpet and into the living room. She could smell it too, like an open sewer. Wayne, Janis and Dean rushed out to the hall and left Maddie and the children alone with Stu and his elderly parents.

Maddie watched the dark stain of the water creeping towards them. The smell of shit grew stronger.

'Help me get Mother out of here,' Mac said.

Stu and Mac stood either side of her chair and, gripping her by her arms, manoeuvred her to her feet.

'Come on, Mum, let's move you into the kitchen where it's a bit drier.'

Maddie looked up at Stu and pointed at the encroaching water. 'Are you going to make us sit in that?'

Stu picked the gun off the coffee table. 'No. Let's go in the kitchen. Turn right out of here and then it's your first door on the right. We'll be right behind you.'

Maddie clambered to her feet. Jessica and Oliver stood up, and Maddie held their hands.

'Go on.' Stu waved the gun at the open door.

Holding her mother's hand, Jessica stepped out of the living room first, followed by Maddie and then Oliver. Brown water gushed out from the toilet and across the hall. The floor felt spongy beneath Maddie's feet. In the kitchen Wayne was on his knees and his head and shoulders were inside a kitchen cabinet beneath the sink. Janis and Dean were nowhere to be seen.

Stu entered the kitchen with his parents and indicated that Maddie and the children should sit at a small dining table.

'You found that stopcock yet?'

Wayne grunted and his voice sounded muffled from inside the kitchen unit. 'Fucking thing's jammed open.'

Maddie noticed the kettle, steam trickling from the spout. Janis must have filled it to the top with water, the indicator said it was still half-full.

Stu had his back to Maddie as he watched Wayne and supported his mother's arm.

On the kitchen counter sat a knife block. One black handle protruded from it.

Jessica touched Maddie's hand. Maddie looked at her, and she gave her mother a jerky little shake of her head.

Jessica was right, it would be suicide to try anything like that. But these people were going to kill them anyway, Maddie was sure. They were waiting for someone to arrive and tell them what to do, that was all. Who was that? And what did they want from Maddie?

There was no time to think about that. They had to do something before he arrived.

Stu and his father helped the old woman onto a kitchen chair. Still she chewed and chewed, gazing disinterestedly at Maddie and the children.

Stu stepped closer to Wayne. 'Where are Janis and Dean?'

Wayne spoke, his voice still muffled from the inside the cupboard. 'They're outside, trying to find somewhere to turn the water off.'

'Fuckin' hell, Wayne, why can't you go to the toilet regular, like everybody else? Fuckin' place smells like a shithouse.'

Maddie's hand seemed to have taken on a life of its own as it crept towards the kettle, just within reach. Jessica tugged at her sleeve, but Maddie knew she had crossed a threshold.

It was too late to stop now.

Maddie leaned forward and grabbed the kettle. With her thumb, she flipped open the lid. Rising from her seat, she swung the kettle at Stu. The hot water poured from the kettle and over Stu's head and neck.

He screamed as the hot water scalded his flesh. The gun fell from his lifeless hand and he spun around to face Maddie.

She threw the rest of the hot water in his eyes. Stu screamed again and his hands flew to his face. He sank to his knees and Maddie smashed the kettle against his head. Still clutching his face, Stu folded at the waist and sank to his elbows. Maddie hit him again and again. With each blow the kettle grew more dented and mangled.

'What the fuck's happening? Stu? Stu?' Wayne's backside wiggled as he started edging his way out of the tight cupboard. 'Stu?'

Maddie dropped the kettle on Stu's head. He was flat out on the kitchen floor now, moaning incoherently.

Maddie spun around to face Mac, who had risen from his chair, his mouth open, his eyes wide and the pupils like pinheads.

Maddie slid the kitchen knife from the knife block.

Mac sat down again.

Maddie stepped over Stu, clutching the knife blade forward. With one powerful thrust she sank the blade into Wayne's bottom, right between his butt cheeks. She shoved the blade in deep until it had disappeared up to the handle. A patch of red bloomed in his blue jeans, spreading across his buttocks.

Wayne screamed and banged his head against the underside of the sink. His body began trembling as he screamed again. One hand appeared from inside the cupboard, fingers scrabbling at the air, trying to find the knife.

Maddie turned to face her children. They stared at her with wide eyes, their faces as white as sheets.

'Run!' Maddie hissed.

Chapter 9

Jessica and Oliver stared at Maddie as though she was the psycho here. Maddie could see it in their faces. What the hell had their mother just done?

Maddie grabbed them both by their shirts and hauled them off their stools. 'Run!'

'What the fuck?'

Dean stood in the open kitchen doorway, surveying the damage. Stu lay face down on the wet floor, the mangled kettle beside his head. Wayne's backside was still the only visible thing of him protruding from the cupboard. A high-pitched keening noise came from inside the cupboard. Dark blood flowed down his legs and mixed with the brown water seeping into the kitchen.

Mac sat at the kitchen table, clutching his wife's hand. Mother was still chewing.

Dean reached down and picked Stu's gun off the kitchen floor.

As he raised it, his face transforming into a rictus of hate, he took a step forward. His right leg flipped out from beneath him as he stepped on a piece of brown sludge and slipped. He twisted as he fell and smacked onto the wet floor on his back. The gun flew from his hand and skidded across the floor.

Stu groaned and lifted a hand to his head.

Maddie splashed through the water, running for the gun. Dean sat up and got on his hands and knees. He was closer to the gun than Maddie and she stopped, held back. They stared at each other in a momentary stand-off.

Dean lunged for the gun, arm outstretched as he slid across the kitchen floor on his chest.

Maddie ran at him. As he lifted the gun, swinging it towards her, Maddie kicked him in the face. Dean's head snapped back and blood flew from his nose. Somehow he managed to keep hold of the gun. Maddie grabbed his hand and tried to prise the gun from his fingers.

Janis stepped into the kitchen. 'Oh, fuck!'

The gun fired as Dean's finger jerked against the trigger. Plaster exploded from the kitchen ceiling, showering Dean and Maddie in grey dust. Dean twisted and pulled Maddie down on the floor with him. Still she hung onto his hand holding the gun, dimly aware of cold, stinking water seeping into her clothes.

'Help me!' Dean yelled.

Janis ran towards them, her feet splashing in the sludge.

Dean tried to jerk his hand free of Maddie's grip and the gun fired again. Janis twisted in a sharp motion as her left shoulder exploded in a spray of crimson.

'You shot me!' she screamed.

The gun fired again and a mug on the kitchen counter shattered, spraying cold tea against the tiles.

Maddie let go of Dean's hand and smashed her elbow into his face. His head snapped back. She heard the crunch of his nose. She made another grab for the gun, but still

Dean managed to keep a grip on it.

Staggering over to them both, Janis grabbed Maddie by the hair with her one good hand, and yanked her head back. Maddie grabbed Janis's wrist and tried to release the pressure on her scalp. Janis kicked her in her side and let go of her hair, dropping her in the water, all the while whining with pain.

'Fucking bitch.' Dean climbed to his feet. Pointed the gun at Maddie. 'Tell me why I shouldn't just shoot her in the fucking face right now.'

Janis clutched her bleeding shoulder. 'Just do it, Dean, fucking do it.'

A muscle in Dean's tattooed neck twitched and jumped. But he hesitated. As much as he obviously wanted to kill her, Maddie realised something was holding him back. They were waiting for someone. Someone with authority, who wanted to talk to Maddie before they disposed of her and her children.

Stu groaned again and lifted his head from the filthy water running over the kitchen linoleum. The back of his neck had erupted in bubbled skin, looked like bubble wrap.

'I can't fucking see.' He rolled over onto his back. His eyes had swollen shut, the skin purple and blistered.

Stuck half in the cupboard still, Wayne wailed and sobbed. His feet jerked and kicked, but he made no move to back out of the cupboard. Maddie had plunged that knife into his arse as deep as she had been able.

Dean clutched his tattooed scalp. 'Oh God, what a complete fuck up this is.'

Maddie glanced at Jessica and Oliver. They were both

frozen in place, staring in shock at the grisly tableau.

'Oh shit, I don't feel so good.' Janis's face had turned white. The blood running down her injured arm dripped off her fingers and into the water.

Her eyes rolled back. She collapsed, brown water splashing as she hit the floor.

Dean's head swivelled to look at Janis and he lowered the gun. Maddie watched in horror as Jessica, seeing that Dean had his head turned away from her, charged him. Dean heard the noise and turned back, but too late. Jessica crashed into him, grabbing the arm that held the gun and sinking her teeth into his hand.

Dean yelled and backhanded her in the face. Jessica toppled over, smacking into the water.

Maddie scrambled to her feet and grabbed the knife jutting from Wayne's backside. As she pulled it out, Wayne's wail turned into a high-pitched scream and blood jetted from the rip in his jeans.

Maddie swung the knife in a broad arc at Dean, slicing open the flesh on his face. Not waiting to see the damage she had done, Maddie advanced upon Dean, slashing at his face again and again. Dean, his face a patchwork of bloody flesh, tripped over his feet and landed on his back on the floor. He screamed.

Maddie plunged the knife into his neck.

The screaming stopped, replaced by a wet gurgle. Dean grabbed at the knife's handle with both hands. His eyes glazed over and his hands fell by his sides as the flow of blood from his neck began to lessen in its power.

Wayne sobbed inside the kitchen cupboard. Stu groaned and cried. Janis lay on her back, her chest rising and falling but slowing down as her shoulder continued bleeding out.

The sound of water gushing from the toilet cistern was the only other noise.

Maddie stared at her children. This was all her, she had done this. She had killed and maimed these men, and her children had watched it all. Every grisly detail. Maddie took a deep, ragged breath and balled her hands into fists. Dug her nails into the soft flesh of her palms. Chewed at her bottom lip until she could taste blood.

The black cloud of panic and despair that had threatened to engulf her retreated a little.

'We need to leave. Now.'

Oliver nodded. Jessica took his hand.

'Out the back way, quick,' Maddie said.

'Mum, the men who brought us here, they were policemen, they were dressed as—'

'I know, I know, but we need to get out of here, you can tell me everything later.'

Maddie glanced at Mac and the old woman. She was still chewing, but her jaw was working much faster now as she stared at the scene of horror laid out in the kitchen. Mac was clutching her hand.

'Look what you've done.' He glared at Maddie. 'Look what you've done.'

Maddie turned her back on him.

A door at the rear of the kitchen led into a small utility room, housing a washing machine and a mop and bucket. Another door opened to the small back garden, run wild with long grass and weeds. Rain hammered against the ground.

Maddie looked at Jessica and Oliver, neither of them

wearing a jacket. All three of them would be drenched within seconds of setting foot outside.

But the only other alternative was to wait here for the man giving the orders to arrive.

Maddie gripped Jessica and Oliver by their shoulders. 'Listen to me. We have to go now before more of these bastards arrive, because if we are still here they will kill us.'

'Where are we going? To the police?'

'No. I don't know.'

With her children beside her, Maddie stepped outside.

Raindrops pounded against their heads and shoulders, soaking them. Maddie pushed strings of wet hair off her face. Where were they going to go? Maybe Jessica was right, and they should go straight to the police. She had her children back now, they were safe.

But these people weren't the only ones who had told her to not alert the police. The mystery caller, the one who had offered to help, he had said the police couldn't help her.

'Mum?'

Maddie, pulled from her thoughts, turned to Jessica and Oliver. Their faces were drawn and pale, tired eyes wide with fear. Staring at her, waiting for her to tell them what to do.

I don't know what to do. Who are these people hunting us down? Why do they want to kill us? I wish I knew what to do. If only Jonathon was still alive, he would know.

'Mum?' Jessica's bottom lip had begun to tremble.

Maddie squeezed her hand. 'Come on, let's get out of here. Get away from this place.'

'But Mum, Aunt Ellie, she's dead.'

'Not now,' Jessica snapped. 'We've got to move first,

we've got to escape.'

Maddie clutched both her children close and pulled them with her as she waded through the long, wet grass. At the end of the tiny garden a gate led to a footpath running parallel to the street. On the opposite side of the narrow path were more tiny gardens and the backs of terraced houses. Rusted bikes, faded plastic kiddie cars, tumbledown sheds and the occasional fridge and washing machine littered the gardens, protruding like alien artifacts from the tangle of weeds and grass.

Maddie paused on the footpath, looking first one way and then the other. Time was short, they had to get moving before more of those killers arrived. But Maddie had lost all sense of direction. Which way was the train station?

The thump of a car door slamming shut shocked Maddie out of her confusion. Where had that sound come from? The front of the house?

'Run, quick!' Maddie hissed.

It didn't matter which way they ran, they just had to get away. Holding hands, the three of them ran along the path. Fat drops of rain pelted them in their faces. Maddie blinked water out of her eyes as she ran. Apart from the constant drum of the rain hitting the ground, Maddie could only hear their laboured breathing and the thump of her heart.

She glanced back. Her legs almost buckled when she saw a figure stepping onto the path and staring at her. It was hard to make out details in the darkness. Was this the mystery man, the one in charge?

No time to think about that.

Facing forward again, Maddie forced her exhausted

body to run faster.

They reached the end of the footpath. Another deserted street, more terraced houses. Sheets of water cascaded across the tarmac and frothed and bubbled at blocked drains.

A black van turned the corner at the top of the street and accelerated towards them. Its headlights dazzled Maddie.

'Run, as fast as you can, run!'

They stumbled along the pavement. Maddie sobbed.

The van overtook them and squealed to a halt as it mounted the pavement and blocked their path.

A girl leaned out of the driver's window. Purple spiky hair. Studs in her ears and lips and nose.

'Get in the back, quick!'

'What?' Maddie was frozen in place.

The girl opened the door and jumped to the ground. She dragged the side of the van open, sliding the door back on its rails until it stopped. The van's grubby interior had nothing but the stained, dusty floor to sit on.

'Come on guys, get in!'

What other choice did they have?

Maddie pushed Oliver and Jessica into the van and jumped in after them. The girl slid the door shut with a loud thump, and they were plunged into darkness.

Chapter 10

The van's driver seemed to have no concern for her passengers' comfort or even safety. She drove at high speed, swerving and taking corners too fast.

In the darkness of the van's storage space, Maddie and her children were thrown about like dice in a cup. She tumbled across the gritty floor and hit her shoulder against the van's side. Before she could grab hold of anything, she was thrown back again, this time sliding on her side until she smacked into the opposite metal wall.

Jessica screamed.

'Jessica? Where are you? Give me your hand, hold on to me!'

'I can't! I don't know where you are!'

The swaying stopped as the van straightened out. Maddie heard the engine note growing higher as the van accelerated. She got on her hands and knees. Vibrations shivered up her arms and legs.

'Follow the sound of my voice, both of you. Quick, before that mad woman turns another corner.'

'Mum, I don't—'

'Just follow the sound of my voice, I'm right here. Ollie, you too.' Maddie held out a hand, reaching into the darkness. 'Here, take my hand, both of you take my hand, I'm right here.'

Trembling fingers found Maddie's hand and closed around it.

'Ollie, is that you?'

A body pulled itself against Maddie. Arms thrown over her, hands gripping her tight. Ollie.

'Jessica? Keep moving to me, keep following the sound of my voice.' Maddie reached out again. 'Jessica, I'm right here.'

Maddie and Oliver fell over and smacked against the floor in a tangle of limbs as the van suddenly braked. Oliver screamed. Before she had a chance to recover and get her balance, the van was accelerating once more.

Oliver threw his arms around Maddie's neck and hung on.

'Jessica!'

More hands grabbing at Maddie's arm, clinging on as though they were hanging over a vast chasm.

'Here, I'm here, it's okay.'

Maddie pulled Jessica in close and wrapped her arms around both of her children. The van driver was really pushing the speed up now, and Maddie wondered if they were on a dual carriageway, or maybe even a motorway.

Where were they being taken? And who by?

'Mum? I'm scared.'

'Yeah, so am I.'

They were seated close to a wall and Maddie was able to lean her back against it. Rivets and struts poked into her back, but at least it offered her some support.

Jessica snuggled in closer to her mother. Oliver's warm

breath feathered her cheek. How long had it been since Maddie had held her children so close? When was the last time they had shown each other this much affection?

'Mum, they killed Aunt Ellie, they shot her.'

Maddie squeezed Jessica's shoulder. For the moment she couldn't speak. The horrors of the last few hours hadn't fully penetrated her consciousness yet. Her sister murdered. Her children kidnapped. Those four people, all dead or maimed at Maddie's hand.

She was a killer now. She had stabbed and beaten and thrown scalding hot water over them and left them to die.

And she would do it again if it meant saving her children.

She would do it in a heartbeat.

'Jessica, tell me what happened. Tell me everything.'

Jessica said nothing, but Maddie didn't press her to talk.

After some time, Maddie wasn't sure how long, Jessica started talking. At first the story came out in fits and starts, but soon she had finished and Maddie knew everything.

Maddie closed her eyes when Jessica had fallen silent. She swallowed and clenched her teeth. Jonathon and Harry, and now her sister. They were on their own now, there was nobody else, there was nothing else.

The grief crouched deep in Maddie's stomach, ready to pounce and drag her into its depths. And Maddie thought that if she let it, she might never haul herself back. That it would devour her whole.

Maddie filled her lungs with the stale air of the van and shoved that grief into a basement in her mind where she could keep it caged.

For the moment.

'Jessica, tell me, on the drive down here, did that man say anything to you? Did he tell you why they were doing these things?'

Maddie felt Jessica's head against her chest as she shook it.

This was all so senseless and random. What did these people want? There had been four of them at the house and then the two sent to the cottage in Scotland. Then there was the man Maddie had seen on the footpath as they made their escape.

Maddie's breath caught in her chest as a thought struck her. Had the two killers sent to Scotland thought they were murdering Maddie, not her sister? And if it had been Maddie they had killed, would they have let Jessica and Oliver live, or would they have murdered them too?

Maddie had to hold back the urge to scream. If she let go now, the grief, the anger, the frustration would possess her and throw her into a fit of wild, screaming insanity.

Instead, she buried it all in that basement in her mind.

Somewhere she could hold on to all that rage until the time came to set it free.

The van began to slow. The ticking of an indicator accompanied the drum of rain against the van's roof. The van began climbing a slope, slowed and then accelerated, turning right in a broad sweep. They straightened up again, but this time the driver kept the van at a reasonable speed.

Maddie sat up straight. The darkness was all consuming. If only they could see, at least a little.

'All right you two, wherever we are being taken I don't think we are far away. I need you to find something I can use as a weapon, anything at all.'

'But it's too dark,' Jessica said.

'I know, just get on your hands and knees and feel around, see if you can find something.'

'All right.'

Maddie ran her hands tentatively across the filthy floor. She found the wall separating them from the driver's cab and resisted the urge to bang on it and shout, demanding to know where they were being taken. Maddie felt along the metal partition, her fingers exploring the nooks and crannies. There had to be something, anything.

The van turned and Maddie's centre of gravity shifted, sending her tumbling to the floor.

'Mum? Are you okay?'

Maddie's hand closed around something smooth and cylindrical, strapped to a wall.

'I'm okay.'

She ran both hands over it. Her fingers found sharp edges at the top, ridges and holes and something that felt like a plastic strip. A handle, and a nozzle too. It was a small fire extinguisher.

The van took another corner, and then another. Wherever they were headed they were drawing close, Maddie was sure. She let her fingers explore the fire extinguisher, searching for the clip holding it in place. There it was. With a sharp snap it was free, and Maddie pulled the fire extinguisher from its holder.

The van slowed to a stop.

With a life of their own, Maddie's fingers hurried over the nozzle and the handle. She had to make sure she was pointing it away from herself.

'Jessica, Ollie, get behind me now!'

The engine died.

Maddie heard the rustle of her children drawing closer. Hands reaching out again, bodies pushing past her.

The cab door opened and then a moment later slammed shut.

Silence.

When had the rain stopped falling?

Was that faint squeak the sound of footsteps? Like the sound of a trainer on wet concrete. Maddie held her breath, trying to follow the sound as it moved.

It stopped.

The van's side slid open behind Maddie.

'Get away from us!' Maddie screamed as she threw herself around to face the young woman.

Holding the fire extinguisher out at arm's length, she squeezed the trigger. A jet of foam blasted from the nozzle. Someone screamed as the roar of the fire extinguisher ricocheted around the van. Foam splattered against the sides and the floor as well as jetting out of the open door.

Maddie let go of the trigger.

Framed in the van's opening, the fire extinguisher foam lay splattered across concrete. Maddie saw square pillars and what looked like an empty, underground car park. Everything was lit by the yellow glow of lights in the ceiling.

'Shit!' The voice echoed in the concrete space. 'What the fuck did you do that for?'

Maddie's finger tightened almost imperceptibly on the trigger.

'Did you hear me? This shit's gone everywhere, you

could have fucking blinded me.' She was standing to one side, out of view, and out of firing range of Maddie.

'I don't know who you are, or what your plans are for us. For all I know, you're planning on murdering us.'

'Are you serious? I asked you to get in the van and you did. Nobody forced you.'

'We were being chased.'

'Yeah, I saw that. And I rescued you, and this is how you thank me!'

Maddie's finger relaxed a little. The woman was right. Maybe. But Maddie needed to know more. She needed to be sure.

'Who are you? What's your name?'

'Spider.'

'Really?'

'Yeah, really. You got a problem with that?'

'Why did you rescue us?'

'I don't know, I'm starting to wonder why myself.' A pause, sounds of movement and something wet hitting the floor with a slap. 'Alex sent me.'

Maddie considered this for a moment. Did she know an Alex? Not that she could think of.

'Who's Alex?'

'He's the one phoned you, tried to warn you.' Spider stepped slowly into view, arms held up in a gesture of surrender. 'You're not going to shoot me again, are you?'

Maddie got her first good look at their rescuer. Slim, wearing shorts and a white vest top, tattoos running down her arms, all those studs in her face. But she was pretty and, to Maddie's horror, young. Maybe only a couple of years older than Jessica.

She was also dripping wet. A tiny needle of regret prodded Maddie's conscience.

'You seen enough?' Spider said.

'I'm not sure.' Maddie lowered the fire extinguisher but kept hold of it. 'Where's this Alex? Why didn't he come and rescue us?'

'If you'd put the fire extinguisher down, you can come and meet him, and he'll tell you himself.'

'Mum, I think it's okay,' Jessica said.

Maddie placed the fire extinguisher on the van's floor. 'All right, we'll come with you.'

Oliver grabbed Maddie's hand. She gave it a reassuring squeeze.

They climbed out of the van, moving carefully to avoid slipping on the wet floor. Spider led the way through the empty car park to a set of bare concrete stairs. The young woman took the steps two at a time and the others had to trot to keep up with her.

Maddie lost count of how many floors they passed. The stairwell stank of piss. Up they went, Oliver gasping as he struggled to keep up. At first Maddie thought they might be in a multi-storey car park, but as they climbed higher, she realised this was a residential tower block. She caught glimpses through the windows of a rundown urban landscape. Cranes towered over building sites. The Thames was just visible in the darkness. Maddie guessed they were somewhere in South London.

Spider halted at a door. The stairs kept going up, and Maddie wondered how many more floors there were. Spider punched a number into a keypad on the wall beside the door. With a solid sounding click the door opened a fraction and Spider pushed it wider and beckoned the others through. As they stepped through the doorway, automatic lights flickered on, bathing them in a soft, natural light.

They were now in a short hallway that led to another door. To Maddie's right was an elevator, the closed doors stained and yellowed with age.

'Couldn't we have used the lift?'

'It's broken.' Spider pushed past Maddie and keyed in another number into another security lock.

They stepped through this second doorway, and Maddie had to catch her breath. The space opened out to reveal a living space with sofas, an expansive TV screen mounted on a wall, and bookshelves stuffed with books.

'Maddie, this is Alex,' Spider said.

A man in a wheelchair rolled to a stop in front of Maddie and held out his hand. 'Welcome.'

Chapter 11

What had she expected? More thugs, like Wayne and Dean? Maddie wasn't sure, everything had been moving too fast to consider the mysterious Alex and what he might look like.

But she hadn't expected this.

'Come on in, all of you, make yourself at home.' Alex spun the wheelchair around in one single, smart move and wheeled away.

'I'll get you some drinks.' Spider pointed to a sliding door. 'You can dry yourselves off in there, and you'll find some dressing gowns if you want to get out of your wet clothes.'

Maddie opened her mouth to speak. She had so many questions. But the horrors of the last few hours, the grief for her sister, had exhausted her. All of a sudden, the act of putting words together into a coherent sentence seemed too difficult to even contemplate.

'Soon,' Spider said, seeing Maddie's confusion. 'Get cleaned up first and then we'll talk, okay?'

Maddie nodded.

One step at a time.

The door slid open automatically as they approached.

On the inside there was a large, square button with a padlock symbol. Maddie pressed it and the door slid closed.

They were in a spacious bathroom. A large shower occupied one corner. There was no shower tray, presumably to allow Alex to wheel himself straight in. This wasn't just a bathroom, Maddie realised. It was a wet room. Drainage points dotted the tiled floor. There was a sink positioned at a lower than normal height. A wide mirror, low shelving with towels, dressing gowns, soaps and shower gels.

But there was no toilet.

'Come on, you two, let's get dry.'

Jessica and Oliver looked like drowned rats. Their clothes clung to their bodies, damp and shapeless. Their bare feet were black with dirt. Jessica's long hair, normally so beautiful, framed her face like curtains. The two children stared at Maddie with dull eyes.

Maddie gave them a towel each. 'Take off those wet things and dry yourselves off.' She pulled two dressing gowns from the shelves. 'These look like they're all one size. Here, put these on when you're dry.'

Jessica and Oliver just stared at their mother some more.

'Yeah, I know.' Maddie ran a hand through Oliver's damp hair. 'You both look exhausted.'

'Mum?' Jessica said. 'Shouldn't we go to the police?'

Maddie nodded slowly. 'We will, yes. Soon. Let's just get cleaned up first and find out what's going on here.'

Maddie turned her back on the children and stripped off. She dried herself and pulled on the soft dressing gown.

'Are you guys done yet?'

'Yes, we're dressed.'

They all turned around again to face each other. Jessica

had rubbed her hair dry and already she looked much better, as did Oliver. Nothing could disguise the blank expressions of exhaustion and grief on their faces, though.

Back in the living area, mugs of tea and hot chocolate had been placed on a coffee table.

Spider shrugged, and said, 'I didn't know what you'd want.'

'These are fine.' Maddie sat down and picked up the mugs of hot chocolate and handed one to Oliver and one to Jessica. They sat down next to her on the sofa.

Spider perched on the edge of the sofa opposite. She had changed her clothes, another pair of shorts and a T-shirt.

Maddie took a moment to let her gaze wander over the bookshelves crowded with books.

This room had no windows, she realised. And neither had the bathroom.

Alex appeared, positioning his wheelchair next to the sofa that Spider had sat on. Now that she had time to take a better look at him, Maddie could see that Alex was much older than Spider. Maybe late forties, or very early fifties. His salt and pepper hair was cut short, and he had a body builder's physique, his upper arms like tree trunks. He wore a simple white T-shirt, fitted to his muscular chest and flat abs.

'All right, you feel better now, yes?'

'I will when I know what's going on.'

Alex leaned forward, forearms on his thighs. 'You've been through a lot in the last few hours, I know. How on earth did you escape from the Mulvaney's house?'

Maddie stared at Alex, her mind numb with everything that she had been through.

'Maddie,' Spider said, 'I was there to try and get you out, to rescue you. The last thing I had expected was to see you outside and running. What happened in there?'

Maddie took a deep breath. She told them everything.

When she had finished, Alex tipped his head back and said, 'Wow. The Mulvaney family have been renowned as the most vicious killers in south London for decades, and you took them all out single-handedly.'

'Now your turn,' Maddie said. 'How did you know my children were in danger?'

'I think maybe I should start from the beginning. You've been noticed, Maddie, by some very dangerous people. The Mulvaneys are only the tip of the iceberg, I'm afraid. I'm not sure how far all of this goes back, or how it started, and I'm hoping you can help me with some of that.'

Maddie leaned forward too. 'What do you mean?'

'Let me ask you a question. Why have you suddenly developed an interest in Edward Porter?'

For a moment, Maddie couldn't quite process the question. 'I... don't have an interest in him at all.'

Alex raised an eyebrow. 'That's not what your internet history is telling us. Over the last two weeks, your IP has recorded hundreds of hits on sites about Porter and the British Values party. Hundreds and hundreds of them.'

'That's not...' Maddie closed her eyes.

Oliver, screaming at the television. Edward Porter on the news.

'Ollie?' Maddie opened her eyes, looked at her son. 'Was that you? Have you been running searches on Porter?'

Oliver dropped his gaze. Said nothing.

'Oliver?' Alex said.

Maddie rounded on Alex, a sudden anger flaring inside her chest. 'Don't you talk to him! If you know so much about us, then you know he can't answer your questions, so you just leave him alone. Okay?'

'I apologise.' Alex held Maddie in his gaze.

The anger subsided a little, draining from her chest and leaving behind an empty, blank misery. 'Besides, what has that got to do with any of this? With... with...' She couldn't bring herself to utter the words. *With the murder of my sister.*

'We're not sure yet. Come with me.' Alex turned the wheelchair and wheeled it towards a blank door at the rear of the comfortable living space.

The door slid open automatically as Alex approached.

'It's okay, go on,' Spider said.

Maddie got up and followed Alex.

As she entered Alex's lair, and that was the word that sprang to mind as she stepped through the doorway, his *lair*, Maddie wondered if she was asleep and dreaming. Three large screen monitors dominated the room, each bolted to a separate wall. One of the monitors was dark, another displayed a bright blue screen with lines of white text running down it. The third monitor, the one Alex wheeled himself to, had a social media site on it. Maddie didn't recognise it.

Alex switched tabs on the web browser.

A photograph appeared on the screen and Maddie recoiled, her heart hammering in her chest.

'Sit down,' Spider said, taking her by the arm and guiding her to a chair. She got two more chairs for Jessica and Oliver. All of them were office chairs on wheels.

'I see you recognise him, even though he was at least ten years younger when this photograph was taken. Mac Mulvaney, one of London's most vicious hit men for hire. It's a shame you didn't kill him too, as I am afraid he will be after you now.'

'I didn't intend killing anyone, I'm not a murderer.'

'No, of course not.'

'You still haven't told me what's going on here, how all of this involves me and my family.'

'Your internet search history, or rather Oliver's search history, was noticed. Alarms were triggered at the unusual amount of hits that Edward Porter was getting.'

'Surely that's not unusual. Isn't he tipped to be our next Prime Minister?'

'Unfortunately, yes.' Alex paused. 'Maddie, are you aware of online, targeted advertising? Using the data that tech companies such as Facebook and Google hold on us, anyone with the skill set needed can advertise to very specific groups of people, targeted not only by region, but by age, religion, culture, interests, almost anything you can think of. Remember Brexit? Trump? These were the kinds of techniques that persuaded voters to think the way that they did. The British Values party has been modelling their own campaigns on these techniques, but they have taken it to a whole new level. They have data centres across the country, filled with staff devoted to guiding the conversations online and monitoring the traffic. Yes, your internet search history was a blip in a sea of information, but it was an unusual blip.'

'So what? How does that finish with my children being kidnapped and my sister...?' Maddie's voice failed her when it came to the word *murdered*.

'Alex noticed that the Mulvaneys had been receiving money,' Spider said. 'It looked like they had been paid a deposit for a job, so I got in with Dean, chatted him up one night at a club and went back to his place. I've been hanging around for a couple of days waiting for something to happen, and then this morning Stu and a mate of his set off for Scotland.'

'It wasn't until later that day that I made the connection between that and your search history on Porter,' Alex said.

Maddie held up her hands. 'Hold on, hold on, I don't get it. What has the British Values party got do with those psychopaths?'

Alex leaned forward in his chair, his biceps bunching as he flexed his arms. 'I don't know, Maddie, but the BV party is funded through a complex maze of shell companies and dormant limited holdings, which I am still trying to get to the bottom of. That transfer of money to the Mulvaneys came from that same system.'

Maddie scrubbed at her face and ran her fingers through her hair. A wave of exhaustion flooded her system.

'Let me get this straight in my head. Those two men, it was me they were after really, wasn't it? But I wasn't there, so they brought Jessica and Oliver to London as hostages to get to me. But how did they know where I was? How did they get hold of my number?'

'Aunt Ellie must have told him,' Jessica said, quietly. 'She thought he was a policeman, and he asked her all sorts of questions about you and where you were and how he could get in touch.'

Maddie took Jessica's hand and squeezed it.

'Maddie, may I ask, what are you doing in London?' Alex said.

'Oh.' Maddie's eyes widened. 'I was here to meet someone. Simon Revel-Humphrey, he—'

'He's dead,' Spider said.

'No. I... I spoke to him this morning, via email.'

'He died of botulism poisoning yesterday. There's been a localised outbreak.'

So much death and violence. Maddie's mind whirled with the events of the day. Even as she was travelling south, two hitmen were travelling north to murder her family, and Revel-Humphrey was dying. Were they connected? Revel-Humphrey had wanted to talk to Maddie about Jonathon. But how was Jonathon involved in this?

'Maddie?' Alex wheeled his chair closer. 'What are you thinking?'

Her eyes focused on Alex, who was staring intently at her. Again she noticed his muscular arms and shoulders. Did he have a personal gym here? Now she saw faint scars running down his arms and another down the right side of his face.

As if aware that he was being scrutinised, Alex backed away.

'You know what I'm thinking?' Maddie twisted her head, looking at the high-tech equipment surrounding them. 'I'm thinking, where did you get the money to fund this hideaway? It's like the Bat Cave in here. You two, the pair of you, you're Batman and Robin. A couple of crime fighting superheroes hidden in your fortress at the top of a tower block in South London.'

'You're making fun of us,' Alex said.

'I am just trying to find out what the hell is going on!'

'Calm down, Maddie, we're just trying to help,' Spider said.

'Oh, really? My sister has just been murdered...' Maddie paused, took a breath, she'd said it, *said that word*, '... my children were kidnapped, and I had to maim and kill four people to get them back and now we're on the run, and all you two can talk about is the election and fraud. I don't even know why I am here, I should have just gone straight to the police.'

Maddie stood up.

Alex wheeled closer. 'What are you doing?'

'What I should have done as soon as I got out of that house, I'm going to the police.'

'You can't.'

'Why? Am I a prisoner here now?'

'Of course not.' Alex paused. 'But going to the police would be a foolish decision. One you might not live to regret.'

'And what the hell is that supposed to mean? That you and your crazy girlfriend here will be after me too?' Maddie turned to Spider. 'Look at him, he's old enough to be your father, your grandfather even. Can't you see how creepy this looks? Is he forcing you to stay here with him for sex?'

'No, I'm not exactly his type,' Spider said.

'You're not...' Maddie turned back to Alex.

'Maddie, you are free to go whenever you want, as is Spider. But you are safer here than if you go to the police. The Council has tendrils of corruption everywhere. You will be found and you will be killed.'

'The Council.' Maddie sat down again. 'What the hell is the Council? Is this a conspiracy theory type thing? Are you two even crazier than I thought?'

'Hey!' Spider jabbed her finger at Maddie. 'You should show a little more respect and gratitude. We got you out of that hellhole and we've given you and your kids protection. We're trying to help you here, and all you're doing is throwing a hissy fit!'

'Hey, everyone calm down, look at this.' Alex pointed at a monitor on which the news was playing. A photograph of Maddie appeared on the screen.

'Madeline Graves is missing and wanted for questioning over the attack on the Mulvaney family. A man and a woman have died at the scene of the attack and two more men are in hospital with life-threatening injuries.'

'They're blaming me for that?' Maddie stared at the screen, unable to believe what she was hearing.

'Madeline Graves' sister was also found dead at Mrs Graves' home in Scotland earlier this morning. Police believe the two deaths are connected and are appealing for Madeline Graves to come forward. The public are advised to contact the police if they see her, and to not approach her as she is considered dangerous.'

Maddie closed her eyes. 'I can't believe this. None of this can be happening, it can't be.'

Chapter 12

The day of the argument, Maddie had stormed from the house like a toddler having a tantrum. Today was the day that Jonathon had arranged to work from home, and juggle work with looking after Harry. This day had been months in preparation. Feeling trapped, Maddie simply wanted some space to herself. A taste of freedom. Even his boss had become involved, insisting that Jonathon take some time at home.

And so he agreed, until the day came around and he changed his mind over breakfast.

'I need to go in to the office, Maddie. There's a problem at work and I need to be able to put all my concentration to it, which I won't be able to if I'm looking after Harry.'

Maddie placed her slice of toast on the plate. Her fingers were sticky with honey.

'No. You're not doing this today, not when you promised.'

'But Maddie, this situation—'

'There's always a situation, Jonathon! Always a problem that needs sorting, that needs the attention that only you can give it. You promised.'

Jessica had been chatting to Harry, making him giggle with a stream of nonsense words. Now she fell silent. Maddie hated this, arguing in front of the children. She detested herself and her needs, the way she felt trapped by her family, tethered to the ground when she should have been flying.

'Maddie, you don't understand.'

'Oh, I understand perfectly.' Maddie stood up. 'Jessica, are you ready for school?'

'Yes, but it's early yet.'

Maddie continued staring at her husband. 'Grab your school things, we're going now.'

'Maddie—'

'Don't forget to check on Oliver, if his temperature is still high he'll need another dose of Nurofen at eleven o'clock.'

Those were the last words she had spoken to Jonathon. Maddie had kissed Harry on his head as she left, and that had been the last time she saw her little boy alive. What would have happened if she had given in to Jonathon and let him go to work? Would she have died that day, at the hands of those two drug addicts? Would Jonathon be on the run now from people intent on killing him? Would Jonathon be wanted by the police in connection with the attack on the Mulvaneys?

Spider pulled on a black hoodie.

'Where are you going?'

Spider grinned. 'To Simon Revel-Humphrey's house for a spot of breaking and entering.'

'Are you serious?'

Alex wheeled closer. 'Revel-Humphrey obviously had something important to tell you, and he didn't want do that over the phone or via email. We need to find out what that was.'

'His wife and kids are staying with relatives, and so the house is empty right now,' Spider said. 'We won't get an opportunity like this again.'

Maddie stood up. 'I'm coming with you.'

'No,' Alex said. 'You should stay here, it's too risky. Spider knows what she's doing.'

'I don't care, I'm going. I'm sick of being on the run, of hiding and doing nothing.' Maddie stepped up to Spider. 'I'm coming with you.'

Spider scooped up the van keys. 'All right, but you do exactly as I tell you when I tell you, okay?'

'Yeah, sure.'

'Mum? Are you leaving us here?' Jessica glanced at Alex.

'You'll be fine,' Maddie said. 'I'll be back soon.'

Maddie followed Spider out of Alex's lair (she couldn't think of it as anything else) and down the concrete stairs. Their footsteps echoed in the empty space. Through the rain smeared windows, Maddie saw the city lights.

Spider drove north and Maddie watched out of the van's window as the landscape changed from run down and industrial into a more upmarket character. Alex had given Maddie a pre-paid mobile phone. The device was tiny and plastic and it had small, fiddly buttons, but at least she could contact Jessica and Oliver if she needed to.

Spider slowed the van to a stop and turned off the headlights and the windscreen wipers. The van was parked on the side of a country lane and beneath the covering of a large tree. The rain still fell, and drops of water splatted onto the windscreen from the branches overhead.

'Revel-Humphrey's house is a couple of hundred yards up there,' Spider said, indicating the road ahead where it disappeared to the left around a tight bend. 'We'll go in from the back, through the garden.'

'What about security lights?'

'As long as we keep in the shadows and out of sight, it won't matter if we trigger them. They go on all the time out in the countryside, foxes and rabbits trigger them a lot. They might even be switched off.'

'Okay.' Maddie took a deep breath.

'You all right? You sure you want to go through with this? You can stay here if you want.'

Maddie shook her head. 'No. Let's do it.'

They left the van and its protection from the rain and made their way through the woods. Maddie's shoes squelched in pockets of mud and her feet were soon wet. Spider led the way. The woodland was sparse and they could see orange lights glowing from the houses on the other side. These were huge, detached houses with extensive gardens. The village was on a commuter run into the city, and a favourite amongst politicians and City of London CEOs.

Both Maddie and Spider were outfitted entirely in black. With their hoodies pulled up and hiding their faces, Maddie expected they looked just the part of burglars. As long as they weren't discovered, that would be fine, as the whole point of the outfits was to keep their identities hidden from any CCTV installed at the house.

A low fence divided the public land from Revel-Humphrey's back garden. They climbed over it and ran, crouching, down the side of the garden towards the wide patio. The rain pounded Maddie's back and head. They passed a shed and a summer house.

The security light flicked on, flooding the garden with bright, harsh illumination.

Maddie and Spider shrank into the shadows of a hedgerow. If Spider was right about how often the security lights were triggered out here, then the neighbours would probably not bother to look out of their windows. Even so, Maddie found herself holding her breath as they waited for the light to switch off.

Several long moments later they were plunged into darkness once more.

'I can't see a bloody thing!' Maddie hissed.

The after-image of the bright light obscured Maddie's vision.

'Just wait,' Spider murmured. 'Let your vision come back.'

'But won't the light come back on as soon as we start moving again?'

'Not if we keep low and in the hedge. We just need to take it slow and careful now.'

Finally their vision returned and Maddie could see the dark shapes of garden furniture and the outline of windows on the rear of the house. They crept through the bushes on hands and knees.

On the patio they crept down the side, hugging the garden fence, brushing past wisteria dripping with rain water. They made their way to a large conservatory. Spider produced what, to Maddie, looked like a wallet and opened it up. Inside were silver tools laid out in a row.

Spider crouched by the conservatory door and inserted

two of the slender tools into the lock.

'Have you picked a lock before?' Maddie whispered.

'Nope, this is my first time.'

'Seriously?'

Spider popped one of the slender picks between her lips and produced a third. 'No, I've done this hundreds of times.'

Maddie swallowed the urge to bite back with a snappy reply. This wasn't the time or place to be having an argument.

The seconds stretched out as the rain fell on them. By now Maddie's clothes were drenched through. She might as well have submerged herself in a bathtub full of water.

'Are you sure you can do this?'

'Just shut up and let me concentrate,' Spider muttered, the pick in her mouth wobbling as she spoke.

Maddie bit her lip. What had she thought she was doing when she insisted she come out here? She was already wanted for the killing of Janis and Dean, even if it was self-defence. How inclined would the police be to believe her if they caught her breaking and entering?

The security light burst into life, illuminating the garden with its bright, harsh light. Spider froze, her eyes wide. Maddie knew how she felt. They were both facing the conservatory and had their backs to the garden. Something had triggered the light. Was there someone standing behind them? Had they been discovered already?

Slowly Maddie turned her head, expecting to see a row of policemen with guns and handcuffs at the ready. Instead she saw a rabbit on the lawn, frozen in the glare of the security light. Its nose twitched, and it sprang into life, hopping into the hedgerow and disappearing.

'It's just a rabbit,' Maddie whispered.

'Thank God for that.' Spider returned to working on the lock.

Several hideously long moments later, the light turned off.

Spider paused in her work and lowered her head.

'What's wrong?'

'I can't see again.'

'We should go before we're discovered. Let's leave it now and get out of here.'

'No,' Spider said. 'I can get in here, I just need a moment.'

'A moment?' Maddie hissed. 'You've had several moments already. How long's this going to take?'

Spider lifted her head and started work again, holding one of the picks in place as she slowly, tenderly twisted the second one.

Maddie heard the faint click of the lock and saw the smile on Spider's face. 'There, done.' She turned the handle and pulled the door open.

Maddie was grateful to step inside the shelter of the conservatory. The rain drummed against the roof and she dripped on the carpet.

'Won't there be an alarm?'

'In the main house, yes.'

'The main... oh, right.'

Spider was already kneeling down in front of the next door, her lock picking tools already in the lock. This second door didn't take as long as the conservatory door had done, as though Spider was getting warmed up now and more confident. Perhaps the fact that she was sheltered from the heavy downpour helped her concentration.

'I can't believe that a house like this would have a door with a lock on it that can be picked so easily,' Maddie said.

'You'd be surprised. Most locks are designed using the same system of tumblers and levers, which means that no matter how expensive they are the system for picking them remains the same.'

Spider opened the door and Maddie tensed, waiting for the insistent beep of an anti burglar system warning the home owners that the alarm was about to start up unless they keyed in the correct security number.

Nothing happened. The house remained blissfully silent.

'What's happened? Why hasn't the alarm gone off?'

'I'm not sure. Maybe the wife just forgot to set it, or maybe Alex hacked into it and turned it off remotely.'

'Can he do that?'

'I don't know.'

They stood in silence, waiting for the alarm to start, or for blue lights to swoop across the back garden.

Nothing.

'Come on,' Spider whispered. 'Let's find Revel-Humphrey's office.'

They crept through a vast living room, leaving behind damp footprints in the lush carpet. A cold, dead log burner stood in the massive fireplace. Bookshelves, tall enough that a ladder would be needed to reach the top shelves of books, lined one wall. A huge bay window at the front looked out onto a garden and a drive down to the country lane. The curtains had been left open.

They stepped out into the tiled hall. A broad staircase swooped upwards. Spider pointed to a door opposite them, at the foot of the stairs. Her intuition was correct, and they stepped into a home study.

Spider pulled the curtains closed and turned on the light.

'Shouldn't we leave the light off?' Maddie said.

'No, we're going to look far more suspicious waving a torch around in the dark.'

Spider went straight for the computer and tapped the space bar on the keyboard. The monitor sprang into life with a photograph of Revel-Humphrey and his wife and two young children. A pang of guilt twisted in Maddie's chest as she realised they were invading this family's house at a time when they were vulnerable and grieving.

Spider sat down at the desk. The computer was asking for a password.

'Search the office, see what you can find,' Spider said.

'What about you? How are you going to get into his computer without the password?'

'I can't, but Alex can. Take a look around, see if you can find anything that might be useful to us.'

While Spider got on the phone to Alex, Maddie began wandering around the office space. Anything that might be useful was a vague enough description to leave Maddie clueless. In the movies the hero always seemed to know exactly what they were looking for. But here, in Simon Revel-Humphrey's office? A man she had never met and had no communication with other than by email.

But he had been insistent that they meet.

Maddie let her eyes wander over a bookshelf. Hardback

books, all political titles or biographies. Some classical history and religion. Next to the bookshelf stood a short, stumpy filing cabinet with two drawers. Maddie crouched in front of the cabinet and pulled at the top drawer, fully expecting it to be locked, but it slid open easily. She leafed through the folders. Correspondence with parishioners, printed emails, press cuttings, nothing that Maddie could see that might be useful.

She pulled at the bottom drawer. This one resisted her attempt to open it.

That made it more interesting.

Maddie glanced at Spider, but she was still on her mobile, reading out a string of numbers from the base of the router. The computer was still waiting patiently for a password.

Maddie looked at the locked drawer. Could she force it open? It didn't appear to be that strong. But what with? She doubted that Simon Revel-Humphrey kept a crowbar in his office. Perhaps the key was somewhere in here.

Maddie pulled a desk drawer open. There was a black plastic tray inside, divided into four compartments. The tray overflowed with pens, paperclips and batteries. Curiously, the drawer also contained a rape alarm, still boxed up and sealed.

Maddie lifted the tray out of the drawer, hoping the filing cabinet key might be hidden beneath it. There was nothing.

She ran her hands along the bookshelf, gathering dust on her fingertips. The key had to be somewhere in here. Surely he wouldn't have kept it on him?

In frustration, Maddie grabbed the cabinet drawer's

handle and yanked at it.

'Need a hand?' Spider said. She had finished talking to Alex, and in her hands she held out the lock picking tools.

Maddie shuffled out of the way, and Spider had the drawer unlocked within ten seconds.

'Those things are easy,' Spider said, and turned back to the computer.

Maddie pulled the drawer open, unconsciously holding her breath in anticipation. She leaned closer to the open drawer and reached inside. She pulled out a porn magazine. More magazines nestled in the drawer. Maddie quickly flipped through them, but there was nothing else there apart from his secret stash of porn.

Maddie slammed the drawer shut.

'Okay, we're in,' Spider said. 'Now, let's see what we've got.'

Maddie stood behind Spider and watched as she browsed through Revel-Humphrey's emails. The headers scrolled by, pages and pages of them, too fast for Maddie to read.

Spider brought up the email server's search bar and typed in 'Madeline Graves'.

The search returned no results.

She typed in 'Jonathon Graves'.

Nothing.

Spider paused. 'You know, I haven't seen any emails to or from you. Didn't you say he was in touch with you by email?'

Maddie leaned in closer to the screen. 'He was, but it wasn't this email address he used.'

'Okay, so it looks like he might not have wanted anyone

else to know he was in touch with you, so much so he was worried his emails might be monitored.'

Spider closed down the email application and hovered the cursor over the folder icon.

'Wait,' Maddie said. 'Look at the Recycle Bin, it hasn't been emptied.'

Spider double clicked on the icon and a new window opened.

'Looks like Mr Revel-Humphrey didn't empty his Recycle Bin very often,' Spider murmured, scrolling down through the files.

She paused. Double clicked on an image file.

When the photograph sprang open, filling the screen, Maddie's stomach turned over. But it wasn't just the sight of her husband staring out of the monitor.

'What is it?' Spider said.

'That's Jonathon, sitting next to Revel-Humphrey.'

'Do you know who that third guy is?'

Maddie nodded. 'That's Bob Willoughby, he was Jonathon's manager.'

And there, sitting next to Willoughby, was Edward Porter. The four men were having a lavish dinner, and were dressed in black tie outfits. The four men were all leaning in, as though the conversation was intense or confidential. Only Jonathon had noticed the photographer and had turned away from the others, looking straight into the camera.

'This wouldn't have looked good for Revel-Humphrey, attending a black tie dinner do with the leader of the opposition. I wonder if this photo had been sent to him as a means of blackmail?'

'I don't know,' Maddie muttered. 'Maybe.'

'Whoever you are, I have a gun, and the police are on their way.'

'Shit!' Spider hissed.

The voice had come from the hall, through the partially open door. A woman's voice, the quaver betraying her fear.

'Keep her occupied.' Spider turned back to the computer and opened up a browser window.

'What?'

'Just keep her occupied for a minute, I need to do something.'

'I can hear you talking in there.'

Maddie turned to the door. Her feet had turned into lumps of concrete and her heart hammered in her chest.

'Please, we don't mean you any harm,' Maddie called out.

Spider tapped away on the keyboard behind Maddie.

'Open the door and step outside,' the voice said.

Maddie dragged her feet over to the door and grasped the handle.

'Don't open the door,' Spider said. 'If she sees us, you in particular, you will be all over the front pages tomorrow. Just keep her talking.'

Maddie looked back at Spider, fingers still running over the keyboard 'What the hell do you want me to talk about, the weather?'

'Forget it, I'm done.' Spider yanked the power cable from the computer and it died.

She stood up, pulled Maddie clear of the door and kicked it shut.

The door exploded inward, showering the women with

shards of wood. The shotgun blast echoed in Maddie's head, leaving her ears ringing. With her hood pulled down, Spider leapt through the doorway. She snatched the shotgun from the woman's hands and scooped a leg beneath her ankles. Screaming, the woman fell on her back on the floor.

'Turn that light out!' Spider yelled.

Maddie switched the office light off.

Spider leaned over the woman on the floor, her head twisted away so that she couldn't be seen clearly.

'We're not going to hurt you. We're leaving now, just lie here and wait for the police.'

Spider took the shotgun with her and Maddie followed her back through the living room and the conservatory. They ran outside, the rain hitting them hard. Maddie blinked rainwater out of her eyes as she stumbled through the garden, illuminated by the fierce glow of the security light.

They tumbled into the van and Spider started the engine. The wheels skidded in the mud at the side of the road as the van lurched into motion.

Maddie slammed her door shut and sank into the seat.

What was she doing? Was this her life now? On the run from the cops? Breaking and entering?

Murder?

Chapter 13

The wind blasted through the canyons created by the towers on the South Bank. Maddie loitered by the river, watching the Thames flow by, its black water inviting her in to finish it all.

A sightseeing boat chugged past, its deck filled with tourists. The boat rocked on the choppy swell of the Thames. One of the tourists, his massive belly hanging low over his waist, snatched at his hat. Too late, the wind plucked it from his bald head and carried it over the river, flipping it this way and that, until finally dunking it in the cold, dark water.

The river had swollen from the recent deluge. The water's power was frightening to see, and Maddie couldn't work out why anybody would want to set foot on a boat and sail on the river today. At least it had stopped raining, although the Met Office was warning of a lot more to come. Storm Betty, already having wreaked havoc on the East Coast of America, was headed straight for the UK.

Maddie pulled the black leather jacket tight and lifted the collar. Last night's muggy temperature had dropped with the arrival of the wind and the rain. Earlier that morning as they left Blackfriars Station and walked down the Thames Path, hungry, tired and suddenly cold, Maddie had experienced a brief spell of dizziness. Spider had taken off her jacket and wrapped it around Maddie's shoulders.

'You don't have to be here, you know,' she'd said. 'You can trust me.'

Maddie nodded.

Spider guided her to a bench and sat her down. 'Wait here.'

Sat on the hard bench, facing the river, Maddie closed her eyes and inhaled slowly. The faint smell of Spider's leather jacket somehow comforted her. Reminded her of her teenage years when she'd been dating a boy who wore a leather jacket just like this one. He'd been the drummer in a crappy little punk band, and Maddie had followed them from gig to gig even though she hated their music.

Spider sat down next to Maddie, two cups of coffee in a cardboard takeaway tray in one hand and a paper bag in the other.

'Here, drink this.'

Maddie took one of the cardboard cups and pulled the plastic lid off. She blew at the steam.

Spider opened the bag. 'And eat this.' She handed Maddie a huge muffin. 'Triple chocolate.'

'Oh God.' With a trembling hand, Maddie placed the coffee on the ground and ripped at the muffin's paper casing. She sank her teeth into the chocolate sponge.

'When did you eat last?'

Maddie shook her head. 'I'm not sure.'

'What about sleep? Did you get any on the train yesterday?'

Maddie shook her head again. Her mouth was too full

of triple chocolate muffin for her to speak.

'No wonder you almost crashed.'

Spider bit into her own muffin, and the two of them ate in silence.

As soon as Maddie had finished eating, she picked up her coffee and sipped at it. 'God, I needed this.'

Spider nodded.

Maddie shrugged the jacket off her shoulders, but Spider stopped her.

'What are you doing?'

'I'm giving you your jacket back.'

'Keep it. You might suddenly feel cold again.'

Maddie pulled the jacket back over her shoulders. 'All right. Thanks.'

'No problem.'

Rubbing the leather between finger and thumb, Maddie said, 'Is this real leather?'

'Yup.'

'That surprises me.'

'Why, do you think I'm a vegan activist? An eco-warrior?'

'I don't know.' Maddie continued rubbing the leather between her thumb and finger. 'I don't know anything about you and Alex.'

'It might be better if it stayed that way, to be honest. Besides, none of it is pleasant.'

'What's that supposed to mean?'

'It means that Alex rescued me when I was going through some really bad shit, but whatever I have been through, he's had it worse. Like, a hundred and ten percent worse, okay?'

From her tone of voice the signal was clear; Spider was shutting down this particular conversation.

The abrupt blare of a boat's horn on the river dragged Maddie back to the present. She turned her back on the river and leaned against the railing. Ahead of her now was the old power station that had been transformed into an art gallery, the Tate Modern. Inside its labyrinthine passages were several floors of galleries, a cinema and a cafe. The cafe was situated on the ground floor and laid out in an L shape. It had floor to ceiling windows along its two outward facing sides. This was why Alex had chosen the Tate Modern cafe for their meeting with Willoughby; not only was it a crowded, public space but with the large windows on two sides they were highly visible.

'Spider should be the one to meet with Willoughby,' Alex had said.

'Absolutely not.' Maddie had to control the urge to yell at Alex. A vat of noxious anger bubbled inside her chest and she had to work hard to keep it from boiling over. 'Bob Willoughby was more than Jonathon's boss, he was a friend of the family. He came to the funeral, he...' Maddie paused, swallowed the bile rising in her throat. 'I need to find out if he had anything to do with Jonathon and Harry's murder.'

'And we will find out. But think about it, Maddie, you can't go calling Willoughby and asking to meet up when you're wanted for the attacks on the Mulvaney family.'

'But we've got the photograph of him with Porter.'

'Yeah, but we don't know how significant that is.' Spider flopped down on the sofa. 'And if he is involved, then he already knows everything, including reporting you to whoever is behind all this.'

'But how are you going to persuade him to meet with you?'

Spider's phone pinged. She looked at the screen and smiled. 'He's already persuaded'

A teenager on a skateboard zipped past Maddie, the rumble of the wheels and the closeness of the contact pulling her back to the present.

Maddie glanced to her left and her right, looking for Spider. The young woman was nowhere to be seen, which didn't surprise Maddie one bit. Spider had told her before they left that Maddie should keep out of sight, but Spider obviously had sneaking around down to a fine art.

The plan was that Spider would meet Willoughby in the Tate Modern cafe and attempt to find out exactly what he knew. It seemed like a lame plan to Maddie, who suggested that they lure Willoughby into a darkened alley somewhere and then kick the shit out of him until he confessed to everything.

The fury with which that thought hit Maddie surprised her. All her life she had despised violence, and yet here she was wishing vicious harm upon Bob Willoughby. It was the anger inside of her, she'd never experienced anything like it before.

Alex had managed to persuade Maddie that luring Willoughby to a deserted, out of the way spot where they could beat him up wouldn't work. It might even be that Spider and Maddie would be trapped and then have the shit kicked out of them.

Willoughby had been persuaded to meet with Spider once she emailed the photograph to him. Turned out it was significant after all, enough that Willoughby wanted it kept out of the public domain.

Maddie checked the time on the mobile that Alex had given her. It was a cheap, plastic thing, more like a toy than a real phone, but at least this way she could keep in touch with Alex and Spider.

It was almost time for the meeting. Maddie pushed away from the railing and headed towards the Tate Modern. Spider had told her to keep her distance, but Maddie needed to see Willoughby for herself.

Between the crowds of passersby, rushing along with their heads bowed against the wind, Maddie spotted Willoughby in the near distance. He had on that long, black overcoat of his and his faux-leather gloves. Long strands of hair kept being blown off his bald head, and he kept smoothing them back down. Willoughby had been that way for as long as Maddie had known him, vain enough that he insisted on a comb over in a ridiculous attempt to disguise his baldness.

Maddie waited, letting him order a drink and settle down at a table. Alex and Spider had been right, that was the beauty of the Tate Modern cafe, it didn't matter where you sat you could still be seen from outside. He sat down at a table next to a window and stirred sugar into his coffee. His head constantly bobbed up and down as he looked for Spider.

Maddie had to fight back the urge to run inside and attack him.

There. Spider strode across the plaza, outfitted in black jeans and a black T-shirt. Only the absence of the hoodie kept her from looking like she was about to break in to someone's house again.

Maddie scanned her surroundings. Spider had told her to keep an eye out for anything or anyone suspicious, but Maddie had no idea what she was looking for. All she saw were people battling their way against the wind, students, tourists, a group of school children headed for the Tate Modern.

Maddie turned her attention back to the cafe. Spider was at the counter, buying herself a drink. Did she really have to do that? Couldn't she have just gone straight to Willoughby?

Spider finished paying for her drink and carried the bottle and glass to Willoughby's table. He looked up as she sat down opposite.

Maddie needed to be closer, she could hardly see them from where she stood. But if she drew closer, then she risked being seen by Willoughby. Maddie didn't care, she had to know more.

Stepping out from the concrete pillar she had been hiding behind, Maddie walked up to the Tate's cafe and its wall of glass. Now she could see them better. Spider was leaning across the table, getting right in Willoughby's face. He was leaning back in his chair, recoiling from Spider's intense glare.

What the hell was she saying to him? Had he admitted anything yet?

Unable to take any more, Maddie headed for the Tate's entrance. How could she stand out here, ignorant of what Willoughby was saying, when it concerned her and her children? Maddie pushed her way past a couple leaving the Tate Modern and hurried down the ramp.

She stopped at the bottom. This way led to the Turbine Hall, a massive exhibition space in the centre of the building. The cafe was on the ground floor, which was now above her. Maddie spotted a staircase and ran up it. Through the cafe door, past the counter with its display of salads, sandwiches and drinks.

Spider looked up as she approached and frowned.

Willoughby's eyes widened when he saw Maddie.

He stood up, his thighs banging against the table edge and knocking his cup. White coffee slopped over the edge and pooled on the saucer and the table top.

Maddie planted a hand on his chest and shoved him back in his chair. It rocked back and Willoughby's knees knocked the table, spilling more of his drink.

Willoughby's mouth hung open for a moment. 'Maddie, I—'

Maddie jabbed a finger in his face. 'Shut the fuck up and stay right where you are.'

She sat down.

'What the hell are you doing, Maddie?' Spider hissed. 'I told you to stay away and let me handle this.'

'Yeah, well I couldn't.' Maddie didn't take her eyes off Willoughby. 'I just had to hear what *Bob* had to say for himself.'

'Maddie, I'm sorry, I need to go,' Willoughby mumbled.

'You're not going anywhere, not until you've explained that photograph we sent you.'

Willoughby couldn't meet Maddie's gaze, and he kept his head bowed. 'There's nothing to explain, it was a dinner function, that's all.'

'Oh, really? You and Edward Porter and Simon Revel-Humphrey and my husband? That was quite an unusual dinner date, don't you think?'

Willoughby picked up his cup and stared at what was left of his coffee. Maddie snatched it from his hand and slammed it on the table.

'Talk to me!' she hissed.

Spider leaned in close. 'Maddie calm down, people are looking at us.'

Maddie snapped her mouth shut and took a deep breath in through her nose. Spider was right, if they wound up being asked to leave the cafe it would be more difficult to get Willoughby talking.

'I saw you on the news last night,' Willoughby said, still not looking at Maddie. 'You're a wanted woman.'

'That's right, I am. The carnage in that house?' Maddie prodded her finger in her chest. 'That was me, I did that. Now, you are going to tell me what the hell is going on before I do the same to you.'

The veil slipped away completely, and Willoughby's face transformed from a stricken attempt at bewilderment to a hunted, drawn look. 'You should have run, Madeline, you should have run and kept on running.'

'Tell me, why are these people after me? What did they want with my children?'

Willoughby placed his elbows on the table and plunged his face into his hands. He let out a quiet, anguished moan.

'My children, Bob. You bought them Christmas presents, gave them money on their birthdays. Jessica and Oliver. Those bastards were going to kill them, weren't they?'

Still covering his face with his hands, Willoughby shook

his head and moaned again.

Maddie lunged across the table and grabbed Willoughby's wrists, yanking his hands from his face. 'Talk to me, you pathetic little man!'

Anguished eyes, rimmed with tears, met hers. 'You really should have run, and kept running. They would have found you though, eventually.'

Maddie let go of Willoughby's wrists and sat back in her chair.

Willoughby had lowered his head again, presenting Maddie with a view of his bald, shiny scalp and the strands of hair combed across it.

He mumbled something that Maddie didn't catch.

'What did you say?'

'What are you hoping to achieve, meeting me?'

Maddie leaned over the table, getting right down to his level. 'I want to know why, Bob. I want to know why these people are after me and my children. And why you? What is your involvement in this?'

Willoughby picked up a packet of sugar and ripped it open. He sprinkled sugar granules over what remained of his latte, where they melted and then sank into the white froth. Willoughby shook his head, still refusing to meet Maddie's stare.

'Bob, look at me.'

Willoughby shook his head again.

'You fucking lift your head and look at me or so help me God you will regret it,' Maddie hissed.

'Maddie,' Spider cautioned again, her voice low.

Slowly, Bob lifted his head and looked at Maddie. In his eyes, she saw nothing but fear.

A giggle burbled up from out of Bob's mouth and he snapped his teeth together and sealed his lips.

'You think this is funny?'

'It sort of is, yes.' Bob's face had screwed up into an expression somewhere between laughter and tears. 'Madeline, no one can help you against these people. Not the police, or the army, or the government, no one. Don't you understand?'

Maddie sat back in her chair. Gazed at the spilt coffee dribbling over the edges of the table. 'No, I don't. Tell me, explain it to me.'

Looking back down, Willoughby picked up a paper napkin and began twisting it in his hands. 'I should have listened to Jonathon, he never wanted to get involved in the first place.'

Maddie took a quick glance around the cafe as Willoughby fell silent. He twisted and pulled at the napkin, shredding it into tiny pieces and dropping them onto the table.

Maddie's chest had tightened at the mention of her husband.

'Tell me more, Bob,' she said softly.

Spider leaned in closer to hear what Willoughby had to say.

'It was a chance to make some money, a bit of extra cash, that's all.' Willoughby dropped the shredded napkin and ripped open a sugar packet with trembling fingers. He let the granules scatter over the wet table. 'Nobody would get hurt, nobody would suffer.' He took a deep, ragged breath. 'I offered Jonathon a piece of the action, it was all getting too much for me by myself, I couldn't keep up.' Willoughby looked up. 'And he agreed, Maddie, he agreed.'

'Agreed to what?'

Willoughby bowed his head again. 'Key House Accountancy was given the job of looking after the financial arrangements for the new Thames Barrier project. Simon facilitated a meeting between myself and PivotConstruct, because he was a shareholder, and if it was made public, he would have lost his job as Minister for the Environment. I thought that would be the depth of my involvement, keeping his financial stake in the scheme away from the eyes of HMRC and the government.'

Willoughby paused, as though deep in thought.

'And?' Maddie said.

'There was more to it than that. PivotConstruct are using cheap, sub-standard materials in the construction, and syphoning the extra money away. It was just too much for me on my own, passing the money through shell accounts and off-shore limited holdings. That's when Jonathon became involved. And we were good at it. Everyone was very pleased, and we were earning a nice little extra income.'

Maddie thought of all the promotions Jonathon claimed to have had in those last two years before he died, all the extra money he was earning. Now Maddie knew the truth.

'Is everything all right here?'

The cheerful voice cut through the tension, jolting Maddie back into the world of the present.

A young woman, hair tied back and wearing a Tate Cafe blouse, stood at the table. She had a washing-up bowl and a flannel.

'Let me just clean this up for you.' She began mopping up the spilt coffee and squeezing the liquid into the bowl. She sprayed the table and wiped at it until it was clean. 'Can I get you anything else?'

'No. We're fine, thank you,' Spider said.

The young woman walked away.

'What's the significance of the photograph?' Spider said to Willoughby.

'Our work had been noticed by the people above PivotConstruct.' Willoughby hadn't looked up, and instead stared at his hands as they twisted and fought with each other on the tabletop. 'We were invited to a charity dinner, a black tie do at GridAxis. Simon was there too, and... Edward Porter.'

'Why? Why you four?'

'Because we were all a part of the same project.'

Maddie thought about this. 'That's not right, Porter was leader of the British Values party when the new Thames Barrier was announced. That was a Conservative government project, the British Values party didn't even have a single seat at that time.'

Willoughby twisted his hands together. 'But the money that we were diverting, much of it was funding the British Values party's campaigns and operational costs. That's why they've managed to make so much political ground in recent years.'

'Did you know about this before this dinner?'

Willoughby shook his head. 'No, they told us that night. They said they wanted to involve us even more, Simon too. With his influence in government and our handling of the accounts, they felt that we could go further and faster.'

'And what did you decide?'

'Jonathon was reluctant, he felt we were getting in too deep into some very dangerous waters. But how could we walk away now? We already knew too much. So... we agreed.'

Willoughby covered his face with his hands. Maddie listened to the clink of cutlery, the chatter of the cafe's customers, the hiss of the coffee machines. She exchanged a glance with Spider, who mouthed something at her.

Maddie raised her eyebrows. What?

Spider mouthed the words again. *We need to go.*

Maddie shook her head. Not yet. Not before Willoughby had told her everything.

'What happened next, Bob?'

Willoughby spoke from behind his hands. 'We did as we were told, but then I was summoned to a meeting. They said there were irregularities in the accounts, they said there was money missing. They believed Jonathon was taking a cut of the money for himself.'

An escape plan. Jonathon had been planning on getting out. But how? And where to?

'What did you say?'

'That I had noticed it too. That they were right. I had to, Maddie, I had to say something. But I didn't think they would murder him, I didn't want that.' Lifting his head and taking his hands off his face, Willoughby stared at Maddie. His eyes glistened with tears. 'I didn't want that.'

Maddie screwed her eyes shut. The sounds of the cafe receded into silence. Now there was nothing but Maddie and the knowledge that her family had been targeted for death.

And good old Bob Willoughby had placed them in the spotlight.

Maddie opened her eyes. 'How could you?' She spat the words out like poison. 'How could you stand by and let those bastards murder Harry and Jonathon? How could you attend their funeral, and hug me and say those things, all the time knowing that it was you, you had killed them?'

Willoughby shook his head. 'I... I didn't know what to do, I wanted to say something, I hated myself but you don't know these people Maddie, you don't know what they can do.'

'Were you there, when it happened? Were you?'

Willoughby's eyes widened. 'Of course not. No.'

Maddie resisted the urge to lean across the table and slap Willoughby across the face. No, she wanted more than that, she wanted to punch and kick him until he begged and cried for her to stop. But she had already attracted enough attention by now.

As though knowing what she was thinking, Spider placed a gentle hand on Maddie's arm.

Bob's voice trembled as he spoke. 'Maddie, you don't know these people, you don't know what they are capable of.'

'I've got a pretty good idea.'

'No, you don't. Whatever you have seen so far, whatever has been done, they can do far worse. They're monsters, Madeline, evil fucking monsters.'

'Who are they, Bob? Tell me who they are.'

'I have to go now.' He stood up.

'No you don't.' Maddie got to her feet. 'You're staying right here until you've told me everything.'

'I've already told you too much.' Willoughby pushed past Maddie and walked towards the exit.

Maddie followed, shoving past the customers in the queue and raising a few grumbles of protest. As she hurried after Willoughby, Maddie glanced back and saw Spider standing up.

At the door, Maddie caught up with Willoughby and grabbed him by his arm. 'Wait a minute, damn it! We haven't finished, not until you tell me everything.'

Willoughby wrenched his arm free and pushed his way out of the cafe and onto the concourse. Below them a massive party of school children entered the Turbine Hall, their teachers milling around them and shouting instructions.

'Bob—'

With one last anguished look back at Maddie, he ran down the staircase to the Turbine Hall. Maddie followed him. When she reached the lower ground floor, she found herself engulfed in a sea of excitable children. They swarmed around her, chattering and laughing and ignoring their teachers' pleas to stay together.

Maddie spotted Willoughby heading deeper into the vast Turbine Hall. Pushing her way between the children, she hurried after him. As he passed beneath the bridge connecting the ground floors of the Natalie Bell building and the Blavatnik building, Maddie lost sight of him in a crowd of tourists.

'Year Seven, come back here right now!'

There he was! Maddie rushed forward.

'Ouch!'

Maddie stumbled and looked at the child who had

screamed. A girl, maybe eleven or twelve years old.

'You stood on my foot!' Her face, contorted into an expression somewhere between pain and outrage.

'I'm sorry.'

Maddie looked up again. Willoughby had disappeared once more.

'Miss, this lady stood on my foot!'

'I said I'm sorry,' Maddie snapped. 'Now get out of my way!'

Turning her back on the school girl, Maddie pushed her way through the crowd. She hurried under the footbridge. Before her, reaching up into the cavernous interior of the Turbine Hall, squatted Maman, a massive spider constructed by Louise Bourgeoise. Visitors wandered around its black legs, above them the bulbous spider's body looking ready to pounce.

Maddie hurried between people as they stood, heads tipped back and looking up at the massive spider. She turned this way and that, searching for any sighting of Willoughby.

'Maddie!'

On the bridge stood Spider, pointing, jabbing her finger down and to her right. Running in the direction she had indicated, Maddie saw Willoughby entering the Blavatnik Building.

From there he could exit the Tate Modern on the opposite side of the building from the river and disappear into a warren of streets. Where would he go from there? Back to the Key House Accountancy offices? Or was he going to run and hide? He had obviously been terrified up in the cafe, and Maddie had the feeling that it wasn't her or

Spider he was scared of.

Maddie pushed her way through a revolving doorway and outside.

Willoughby had gone.

Chapter 14

He watched Willoughby running, like the scared little mouse he was. How ridiculous the silly little man looked, with his hair blowing in the wind and exposing his bald patch, and his fat, stumpy legs waddling as fast as they could.

He didn't need to run to keep up with Willoughby. His long, even strides kept him easily in pursuit of his victim. And Willoughby would slow down soon, unable to keep up this pace. Willoughby was a fat little man, used to sitting at a desk all day and snacking while he worked.

Hardly a challenge, this one. Not like Revel-Humphrey.

They didn't care how Willoughby died, how suspicious it might look. Just do it, they'd said. Just do it now, immediately.

It wasn't like them to hand out instructions like this, at the last minute and filled with urgency. Rather inconvenient for him, as he had booked his flight out of London bound for a holiday in Monaco. But now they wanted him to stay, even after he had disposed of Willoughby.

Until tomorrow, the message said. Until after the election.

The inconvenience was a nuisance, but at least he had

been able to negotiate a higher than normal fee as compensation. They didn't care. They had money to burn was what he had heard.

There, that was better, Willoughby had stopped with that ridiculous run. Now he was mopping his forehead with a handkerchief, puffing and blowing like an overworked steam engine.

He hung back, waiting for Willoughby to recover. It would be easy enough to creep up behind the fat man and slide a knife in between his ribs and into his heart. Fun, too. But this street was far too busy. And, although they had said it didn't matter how suspicious Willoughby's death might look, he had the feeling that they would be pleased if it looked like an accident.

Or suicide, perhaps?

It had been a few years since he had last arranged a suicide. It might be fun to see if he could manage one in such a short timescale. After all, he needed to keep his skills updated.

Now, what was that called in today's modern language?

Oh, yes. Continual Professional Development.

He giggled at that.

Willoughby began walking, still mopping his face with the white handkerchief and patting his hair down every time the wind blew at it.

He followed his quarry across Southwark Bridge. Willoughby cast an anxious glance behind him as he walked, but he never once realised he was being followed. People like Willoughby were stupid. People like Willoughby thought they could play with the big boys and not get hurt, that they could swim with the sharks and not get eaten. They soon found out.

And he suspected Willoughby was having a Damascus moment right now. The scales were falling from his eyes and he was regretting ever getting involved. All the money he had earned, all the power he had accrued, none of it meant a single thing right at this moment in time. Willoughby knew he was drowning in an ocean of trouble and he was scrambling for the shore. What Willoughby failed to realise was how far away the shoreline actually was.

Still, he always thought it was good for a man to see the world for what it was before he died. Jesus had said, *The truth shall set you free*. Well, death set a person free too. Imagine that, seeing the truth of the world for the very first time, just moments before stepping across the threshold of death.

Willoughby stepped inside a building on Ludgate Hill.

The Key House Accountancy offices were on the fourteenth floor.

A plan began to form in his mind.

Who the hell was that?

And why was he following Bob Willoughby?

Spider stood at the lights, waiting for the change to green so that she could cross. Traffic was too heavy to dodge across the road, and besides which she could see them down the street opposite. Even at a running pace, Willoughby wasn't exactly a fast mover, and Spider had constantly found herself getting too close.

The pedestrian lights changed to green and Spider crossed the road. She'd spotted Willoughby soon after they lost him at the Tate Modern. She began following him, and it didn't take her long to realise she wasn't the only one on his tail.

As she walked along the pavement on the opposite side of the road from Willoughby and his mysterious pursuer, Spider saw Willoughby enter a glass fronted building. Was that where he worked? What was running through his mind now after his meeting with Maddie and Spider? He had to be in a state of panic still, and he was obviously terrified of the people who employed him. But who was that? Edward Porter? Or the people in the chain above Porter?

Whatever or whoever Willoughby was scared of, it seemed likely to Spider that he would be reporting back. Or maybe, just maybe, he was scared enough right now that he was planning on running.

As Spider drew closer to the building housing the Key House Accountancy offices, she saw the man following Willoughby inside. What was his intention? Was he the police?

Spider's mobile buzzed.

A text from Maddie: Where are you?

Spider's fingers ran over the mobile as she texted back. Following Willoughby. There's someone else following him too. Might be cops. Go back to Alex, I'll catch up with you later.

Where are you? I should be there.

No, too dangerous for you if cops are here.

Spider switched her phone off and slipped it in her pocket. Maddie would have to return to Alex now. Spider could handle whatever happened here on her own, in fact she preferred it that way. Maddie would have been too much of a hindrance.

From her position on the pavement opposite, Spider pondered what she should do next. She only really had two options; wait for Willoughby to come back out and follow him again, or follow Willoughby and the mystery man on his tail inside.

Spider had never been particularly good at standing around and waiting for something to happen.

She crossed the street and pushed her way through the tall glass door.

He found Willoughby sitting at his desk. His face was covered in a sheen of sweat and dark patches stained his shirt beneath his armpits. Willoughby barely registered his presence as he entered the office. This was going to be too easy.

He pulled out a chair and sat down.

Willoughby finally looked up at the intruder in his office. 'Yes? Can I help you?'

He took a moment to regard this man who now only had a few minutes left to live.

'Yes, Mr Willoughby, you can help me. We both work for the same people, and it seems you have fallen out of favour.'

Willoughby swallowed. 'So soon?'

He nodded. 'Yes, so soon.'

'But I can explain. It's not my fault, that woman called me, she was going to expose everything, she—'

He held up his hand for silence. Willoughby took the cue and shut his mouth.

He hated it when they tried to explain their stupid little mistakes away, to try to shift the blame onto others. It seemed that Willoughby hadn't seen the world as it really was, after all. A shame. Maybe he could spend a little time teaching Willoughby before he dispatched him on his journey of discovery.

'Mr Willoughby, or may I call you Bob?'

Willoughby nodded jerkily.

'Well, Bob, your excuses, your reasons, whatever you want to call them, they are of no use to me. I, much like yourself, am an employee. I don't make the decisions, I don't have a casting vote, I don't sit at the table. I'm sure you are aware that there are many levels in the organisation you're are now involved with. Possibly you once thought that you were at a high level, one with responsibility and renumeration equal to your position. I can see you have been disavowed of that rather silly notion now. But, just in case you still hold any ridiculous ideas that you can barter for your life, let me make it clear to you. In the grand scheme of things, you are a maggot. In fact, you're a microbe on the back of a maggot. You are nothing. You are, what's that quaint little saying? Oh yes, you are ten-a-penny, Bob.'

'Really, I—'

'Be quiet.'

Willoughby snapped his mouth shut.

'You say nothing to me, except by invitation. Nod your head if you understand.'

Willoughby nodded his head.

'From this point on, you must have no illusions about your place in the world. You are dog shit, Bob, on the sole of another man's shoe, and that man is dog shit on the sole of yet another man's shoe. And so it goes, Bob. Do you understand?'

Willoughby nodded his head.

'Good, now we are getting somewhere. A little late in the day, unfortunately. I suppose you could say that me explaining all of this to you now is a little like closing the stable door after the horse has bolted. If you had only learned this lesson before today, you might well have lived long enough to be promoted to being the man who has dog shit on his shoe. Your friend Mr Simon Revel-Humphrey forgot that lesson and began to believe he had some measure of power and influence in this world. I corrected him on that point.'

Willoughby gazed blank faced at the man as his brain tried processing the information it had just received.

'I corrected him permanently, Bob. Do you understand?'

Slowly, like mud draining away, the realisation of what this man was saying sank into his mind. 'But, Simon contracted a bad case of botulism, he—'

'Was taken care of. By me.'

All of a sudden Willoughby seemed to deflate, like an old balloon.

Willoughby had seen the world for how it really was.

Willoughby had seen the truth.

At moments like this, he took genuine pleasure in his work.

Still, now wasn't the time or the place to be basking in his success. He had work to do, and there was no time to be wasting in the doing of it.

'Stand up, please.'

Willoughby placed his hands on his desk and pushed himself upright.

'Come with me.'

Together they left Willoughby's office. They passed desks with people working at them, and the receptionist gave them both a smile as they walked by her desk. None of it mattered. His face was a forgettable one. His anonymity was one of his many talents.

Before entering Willoughby's office, he had explored the building and found a route up to the space between the top floor and the roof. Here was hidden the guts of the building's electricity and hot water services. He took Willoughby up the stairs and into the heart of the building's power. Strip lights flickered on the ceiling, the warren of pipes and electrical conduits casting crazy shadows across the floor.

He told Willoughby where to go and walked behind him. Willoughby was docile now, accepting of his fate. When they had reached the space he had found earlier, he told Willoughby to stop.

'Take off your belt,' he said.

Willoughby complied. He had no reason to ask why.

He took the belt from Willoughby and slung it over a pipe running just below the ceiling.

'Step on the box,' he said.

Willoughby did as he was told.

He looped the belt around Willoughby's fat neck and yanked it tight enough that it disappeared into his flabby flesh. Willoughby grunted, his eyes widening with the pain.

He buckled the belt.

He put his mouth by Willoughby's ear.

'It's all over,' he whispered. 'You are free.'

He kicked the box away and stepped back.

Willoughby kicked and grunted as his face turned purple and his eyes bugged from their sockets. His hands flew to the belt around his throat, but the leather strap was buried in the folds of his flesh. Willoughby clawed at his neck. His head looked like it might explode with the pressure.

The kicks grew weaker and his arms flopped by his side and Willoughby fell still.

Satisfied, he turned his back on the dead man.

The girl gasped as she appeared from around the corner, almost colliding with him. Her eyes widened as she saw Willoughby hanging from the ceiling.

Instinct took over. The blade he kept hidden on him slipped into his hand and he slid it into her chest. She sucked in air, her mouth opening wide, and she fell against him. She had purple hair and studs in her face and her breath smelt of peppermints.

Her blood flowed warm over his hand and dripped to the floor. He could feel the tension draining from her body as her life left it.

He lowered her to the floor and laid her out.

Without a backward glance, he headed for the exit, hiding the knife and his bloodstained hand in a pocket.

Chapter 15

'Where's Spider?' Alex said.

Maddie sank into the sofa. 'She stayed back, she's following Willoughby, waiting to see what he does next.'

'She's not answering her phone.'

'She'll be back soon, I'm sure.' Maddie wiped her hands over her face and rubbed at her eyes. 'God, I'm tired. I'm not sure I've ever felt this tired before in my life.'

'You've had an exhausting and traumatic couple of days.'

'Yeah. Where are Jessica and Oliver?'

'They're in the bedroom, I think they might be sleeping.'

'That's good, they need to get some sleep.'

'How did it go with Willoughby?' Alex wheeled his chair closer.

'You were right, Willoughby's in over his head, and Jonathon was involved too. They were responsible for shuffling the money around, taking cash that was meant for the new Thames barrier and putting it into the campaign funding for the British Values party. But Jonathon wanted to get out, and I guess they sent those two drug addicts to murder him.' Maddie looked at her hands lying in her lap. 'And then they murdered Harry too. A couple of days later those two scumbags were murdered by the people who had employed them, and so everything was tied up. There was nothing to indicate that the killings had been anything other than a breaking and entering gone tragically wrong.'

Maddie curled her hands into fists and then extended her fingers out again. That was what had happened, that much at least was obvious. And yet...

Lost in thought, Maddie gazed at the television behind Alex. A shot of Edward Porter with his right-hand man, Brent Kilburn appeared.

There was something wrong. She was missing something. Maddie had the feeling that whatever it was had been staring her in the face for some time now, but she couldn't pin it down, she couldn't see it.

The picture on the television switched to a high level view of London and zoomed in on The Shard. The British Values party had hired an entire floor high up in the iconic tower to celebrate their win.

Money, thought Maddie. That's what it all came down to in the end. That's what Willoughby had said.

The money that we were diverting, much of it was funding the British Values party's campaigns and operational costs.

'Maddie,' Alex said, breaking into her thoughts. 'We need to talk. There are some things I have to tell you.'

'Like what?'

Alex gazed thoughtfully at Maddie. 'Who do you think is in control, Maddie?'

'Control of what? Me? The planet?'

'Both of those.'

Maddie groaned. 'This isn't some kind of conspiracy, secret rulers of the world crap, is it?'

Alex said nothing for a moment, just continued looking at Maddie.

Finally, he said, 'What if it is?'

'Are you serious? If I'd known I was talking to David Icke last night, I wouldn't have stayed. I mean come on, what are you talking about here, shape-shifting lizards? Seriously?'

'Hear me out, Maddie, please.'

'I don't know, this is just too crazy. Look, I already know what you're going to say, I've heard all this conspiracy theory shit before. I don't need to hear it again.'

'Maddie, we gave you shelter and protection last night. Spider helped you today with Willoughby. Please, listen to what I have to say and then make up your mind. Please.'

Maddie's head told her to run, but something about Alex, something in his manner and the tone of his voice, told her to stay. Just for a little longer at least.

'All right, talk.'

'Icke is an idiot, along with all the other conspiracy theorists out there. We all know that if what they are saying is true, they would have been silenced a long time ago before they had the chance to spread their poison. They are narcissistic, attention-seeking idiots.'

'But you're different, right?' Maddie said. 'You know the truth.'

'No, we don't. But we know some of it. Haven't you noticed the rise of extremism over the last decade? And how popular these groups are becoming? The US has already got a virtual dictator established as president, and when we wake up tomorrow morning, the UK will have joined them.'

'Porter? You think he's going to be our next prime minister?'

'Unfortunately, yes, I do. But it's not him that worries me. It's the shadowy web of organisations that are funding him that scares me. They will have more power on the political and economic stage than ever before, and they already have too much.'

Maddie stood up. 'Alex, you might be right, but none of that matters to me at the moment. Right now I just need to find out who is responsible for murdering my husband and son, and bring them to justice. And maybe that way, me and my children can live our lives in safety without the fear of armed men hunting us down.'

Maddie turned her back on Alex and walked towards the bedroom. She was so very tired.

She opened the door.

'Mum!' Jessica jumped to her feet. 'Where have you been? What—?'

'Not now, Jessica.' Maddie threw herself face down on the nearest bed. 'Not now.'

Her world disappeared into darkness and silence.

Maddy awoke groggy and disoriented. She sat up, panic rising in her chest as she gazed bleary-eyed at the unfamiliar surroundings. Then she remembered. Despair washed the panic away.

Oliver was on the other bed, huddled up in a corner, his knees drawn into his chest and his arms wrapped around his legs. Jessica sat cross-legged next to him, holding a sheet of paper.

'What's that?' Maddie said.

Jessica held it out, and now Maddie noticed her eyes damp with tears. Maddie took the sheet and examined it. One of Oliver's drawings. He was a skilled artist and his bedroom was filled with sketches of superheroes and villains, and scenes from his imagination. This sketch wasn't as good as he could do, it was crudely and hurriedly sketched out in ballpoint pen.

But it was unmistakable.

Oliver had drawn the scene as though peering at it through a gap between a door and the door frame. The view was of their living room at their old house in London. Two bodies lay on the floor, and Maddie guessed they were Jonathon and Harry. Another figure stood over them, holding a long-bladed knife. Oliver had coloured in dark splodges of blood dripping from the knife and forming a puddle on the floor in blue ink.

But it was the fourth figure, standing in the background and seemingly there to observe, that gave Maddie the chills.

Were these the drug addicts that murdered Jonathon and Harry? Something seemed off about the drawing. Maddie couldn't quite place it.

'Oliver?' Maddie tore her gaze away from the drawing and looked at her son. 'You came downstairs while the attack was happening, didn't you?'

Oliver hugged himself tighter and refused to lift his head to his mother.

It didn't matter. He'd shown her that he was there with this drawing. The poor child had seen the attack happen, hidden from view behind the living room door.

But what did this drawing mean? Why was it so important that he needed to express it in this way? Was it simply the trauma of the last two days, bringing the event back to life for him?

Maddie examined the drawing once more. Two men, one with a knife dripping blood, another in the background. As if there just to watch.

Was that what was wrong with the drawing? DNA evidence had been found on both the addicts. One of them wouldn't have stood back on the sidelines, surely? They were desperate for a fix.

Was that it?

No.

Maddie turned on Oliver. 'He's wearing a tie, isn't he?'

Oliver stared at his mother.

'That man, in the background, is that a tie he's wearing? Is that what you've drawn, a suit and a tie?'

Oliver nodded.

Drug addicts so desperate for drugs they were willing to resort to murder didn't dress up for the occasion, did they?

Oliver, screaming whenever he saw Edward Porter on the television. His internet search history.

With a trembling finger, Maddie pointed at the sketched figure. 'Is this the politician?'

Oliver nodded.

'Edward Porter?'

Oliver nodded again.

Her head spinning, Maddie sat down on the edge of the bed. She stared at the crumpled sheet of paper in her hand, at the crude sketch. What had Porter been doing in her house? That couldn't be right.

And yet, Oliver had seen him there.

And who was the other man, with the knife?

Maddie raised her head and turned to her son. 'Ollie, I know this is hard for you, I know you don't want to, I know… you can't talk about this, but please, please say something now. Tell me what you saw that day.'

Oliver stared back at his mother. Tears welled up in his eyes and gathered on his eyelashes.

'Dammit, talk to me!' A white hot fury boiled over inside Maddie and she grabbed Oliver's arm. 'Why won't you talk to me?'

Oliver recoiled, trying to break away. But he was trapped in the corner of the room, and his mother's grip was too tight.

'Mum, get off him!' Jessica screamed. 'You're hurting him, look.'

Fat tears rolled down Oliver's cheeks. He turned his head away and refused to look at his mother.

Maddie let go of his arm.

She flinched as she heard Alex scream.

Maddie ran out of the bedroom, into the living area. Alex was gripping the arms of his wheelchair, hunched forward in his seat, and staring at the television.

Maddie knelt beside him. 'What's wrong?'

'They murdered Spider.'

The words slammed into Maddie like a physical blow.

She stared at the television, at the news report.

Bob Willoughby dead, a suicide possibly, found hanging from a pipe in the service area above the Key House Accountancy offices. And a young woman, stabbed to death, lying on the floor nearby.

'You don't know it's Spider, it might be somebody else.' Even as the words left her mouth, Maddie knew how stupid that sounded.

Alex wheeled the chair away and spun around to face Maddie. 'Don't you see now? Don't you see that they are going to murder us all, you, me, your children, and they will keep on killing until they have what they want.'

Maddie shook her head. 'No, no, that can't happen.' That rage, filling her insides once more. 'They have to pay for what they've done.'

Alex tipped his head back and screamed. His whole body trembled with tension. He spun the wheelchair around and wheeled himself into his command centre.

'I'm going to kill them!' he yelled. 'I'm going to kill them all!'

Maddie followed him. A pounding filled her head. It was as though she could feel her arteries pumping blood through her body, as if the sound of it had been caught and amplified a thousand times over.

Alex yanked at a sliding door and pulled it up and open.

A display of guns greeted Maddie's eyes. Alex grabbed a handgun and a box of ammunition. He ejected the clip from the gun and ripped open the box. Bullets cascaded from his trembling hands and scattered across the floor.

Maddie took the gun from him. 'Let me do it.'

Alex stared up at Maddie with wide eyes. 'You? You

can't do this. Have you even fired a gun before?'

'No, but I can learn, can't I?'

Alex's lips peeled back in a dismissive sneer. 'Don't be stupid. Do you really think it is that easy?'

'And you think you can do it, trapped in that wheelchair? You can't even get out of this building without my help.'

Maddie checked the handgun over. She fumbled with the bullets as she pushed them into the clip, one by one. Her hands trembled.

'Stop,' Alex said, his voice suddenly calm. 'Do you even know what you're going to do?'

Maddie paused. 'I'm going to kill Porter. He murdered Harry and Jonathon.'

'He's not the only one.'

'I don't care. I'll start with him.'

'Give the gun here,' Alex said. He took the gun from her and finished loading the clip. 'The safety is here. Make sure to turn it off before you pull the trigger.' He handed the gun back to her. 'You're going to die, you know that, don't you? And if by some miracle you manage to finish the night still alive, you're going to spend the rest of your life in jail.'

'We'll see,' Maddie said.

She strode through the living area.

'Mum?' Jessica called.

Maddie kept walking. 'Go back to your room.'

Jessica got in front of her mother and stopped her. 'Where are you going?'

'Go back to your room and stay there. Look after Oliver.'

A tear rolled down Jessica's cheek. 'Mum, no, don't go, stay here please.'

Maddie took hold of her daughter by her shoulders.

She pushed Jessica out of her way and left.

Chapter 16

With the gun hidden beneath Spider's jacket, Maddie headed into the city. She just had to hope she didn't have to go through any security devices on the way.

She caught the train into the city. The carriages were crowded, and the gun in Maddie's jacket was like a lump of lava, ready to burn its way through the material at any minute and hit the floor, betraying her to everyone in the train carriage.

Maddie kept her arms crossed in an attempt to disguise the bulge, which she was sure was there, and a dead giveaway. But no one spoke to her, no one paid her any attention. The other passengers were more interested in their mobiles, or gazing out of the window at the rain battering the panes of glass.

The carriage had a monitor, and it alternated between news reports, safety announcements, and information about the next stops. The news was all about the election. Despite the heavy rain, and the weather warnings, the city centre was packed with people surrounding The Shard. Supporters and protesters faced off against each other, and the police were out in force.

Another blow for Maddie. The crowds would make it

difficult for her to get to The Shard, and the heavy police presence increased Maddie's risk of being caught carrying a weapon.

None of that was going to stop her.

Maddie changed at East Dulwich and caught the tube in to central London. Again the carriages were packed and Maddie found herself a corner to stand in where she was able to face away from other commuters. As she drew closer to her destination, her sense of exposure increased. How could she have thought that she would get away with carrying a handgun around central London on an election night?

Finally, she reached her stop at London Bridge underground. The train decelerated abruptly. People were crowded together on the platform. This was Maddie's worst nightmare, crowds of people pressing in on her, in tunnels deep underground.

The doors opened and the passengers on the train began fighting their way off. They were met with resistance by people on the platform jostling for space to get on. The queue moved slowly. Maddie hunched herself inward, her shoulders up. She shuffled toward the doors.

On the platform she was pushed and shoved, buffeted like a digital character in a computer game. All the time she imagined the gun falling to the floor, maybe even firing as it hit the ground, the bullets shattering ankles and shin bones.

Finally Maddie reached the escalator, disappearing up to the surface. From there she would climb even higher as she ascended The Shard. Maybe she wouldn't come back down, perhaps she would die up there. Better that way than here, underground.

On Duke Street Hill, the crowds of supporters and protesters had not been put off by the storm. A gale howled between London's towers, driving the heavy rain into people, tipping over placards and snatching them from hands. Still the chants went on. *NOT MY GOVERNMENT!*

Maddie spotted The Shard, its glowing lights a beacon in the darkness. She threw herself into the crowd and the rain. The only way to get past this mass of humanity was to put her head down and bulldoze her way through.

Within seconds she was drenched. The rain ran down her scalp and her neck, and soaked through her shirt. Maddie kept moving, shouldering her way past protesters, ignoring the shouts of anger and outrage.

A hand grabbed her by the shoulder and dragged her back.

A huge man, his dark beard and long hair flattened by the rain. His eyes were narrowed in anger, and he towered over Maddie.

'Watch where you're going!'

'I'm sorry,' Maddie muttered, turning her back on him.

The hand dragged her around to face him again.

'What did you say?'

Now he had both hands on her shoulders, holding her down, pinning her in place. What would he do if he found the gun? Would he use it on her?

The man's lips peeled back, revealing nicotine-stained teeth. Maddie could smell beer on his breath.

She thought about pulling out the gun, shoving it in his fat stomach and pulling the trigger. That would be satisfying.

Instead she kneed him in the balls, putting every ounce of energy and strength into it. The big guy howled and doubled over. Heads turned to see what the commotion was. Maddie slipped into the crowd, becoming invisible once more.

As she drew closer to The Shard, the crush of people intensified. Maddie spotted the occasional patrolling Alpha, but even they seemed a little cowed and unsure of themselves. Blue lights flashed on the fringes of the protest, but Maddie couldn't imagine how the police could react if the protesters got out of control.

Maddie continued fighting her way through the crush of protesters. She caught glimpses of the Thames, the dark water rushing by. Its height had increased.

As she drew close to The Shard's entrance, she spotted the security officers at the door. They were letting someone inside, but they were checking the woman's bag. Would they want to search Maddie? Would they pat her down and find the gun?

Maddie veered off to the side and found shelter. The crowd continued chanting and there were shouts and a minor scuffle. Maddie wiped rain water out of her eyes and smoothed her wet hair back.

Porter was inside that building, and he had to die.

But how was she going to get to him?

A shout of anger attracted her attention. Another scuffle in the crowd. Maddie spotted the big, bearded man who she had kneed in the balls. He must have followed her here, but then lost her. His head twisted from side to side as he scanned the crowd for any sign of her.

Maddie headed straight for him.

'Hey! Doofus!'

His head snapped around, his wet stringy hair whipping across his face. As soon as he saw her, it was as though a switch had flicked in his brain. He tipped his head back and yelled at the dark sky, then he began bulldozing his way through the crowd and straight for Maddie.

Maddie pushed her way past people, shoving at them, pleading with people to move, to get out of the way.

'Someone help me!' she screamed.

Heads turned. Maddie pointed.

'He tried to rape me!'

She backed up. The crowd parted and then closed in again when she had passed through, forming a barrier between her and her pursuer. Her bottom hit the barrier between the crowd and the entrance to The Shard, and she quickly climbed over it.

As she predicted, one of the security guards approached her.

'Get back.'

'Please, help me, don't let him hurt me!'

As if on cue, the big bearded man erupted through the crowd. He lifted his fists and roared, spittle flying from his lips.

'Stand back!' the security guard yelled.

Maddie slipped behind him as the other security guard rushed to his aid.

Perfect.

Maddie stepped into the entranceway. No alarms wailed, pronouncing her a terrorist carrying weapons. The reception desk was empty, Maddie was the only one inside right now.

A line of elevator doors ran along the wall, each of them numbered. Did they all go to all floors, or did some stop at a lower floor than the others?

And there were eighty-seven floors in The Shard. Where would the British Values party HQ be located? Maddie didn't have time to search them all. She punched a big, silver button to summon the lift. Glanced back at the commotion outside. No one was looking her way, the crowd's attention was on the big man who had gone ballistic.

The lift doors slid open.

Maddie stepped inside. Scanned the column of numbers and selected one at random. The doors slid shut, muting the sounds of fighting outside.

The elevator ascended rapidly and slowed to a smooth stop moments later. The door slid open. A wide, empty corridor. Maddie stepped out of the lift. Her wet trainers left dark footprints on the carpet. This looked like it might be part of an apartment. Alex had told her about this, about how there were luxurious apartments built for millionaires, but left standing empty, housed in The Shard. This had to be one of them.

Maddie held herself perfectly still. She could just hear the muted, repetitive thud of music. She craned her head back. They were partying somewhere above her. This was it then, they already believed they had won the election.

Maddie walked over to a large window. Raindrops smeared the glass, but she could still see the city lights of London spread out, like a fantasy world. The lights of the bridge and a single boat navigating the Thames. The river was too fast and powerful for the usual party boats to be out. What was that one boat doing, she wondered.

Maddie turned her back on the window.

She had to find another way into the party going on upstairs. Arriving in the lift would arouse suspicion straight away. There had to be another access point to the various floors. A fire escape.

Maddie ran through the empty apartment until she found what she needed; a fire escape door leading to a utility stairway. As she ran up the stairs, the sound of her trainers smacking against the metal steps, the thud of the party music grew louder.

Maddie arrived at a set of double doors. Through the small rectangular windows she saw multi-coloured lights flashing in the darkness. They were having a celebration all right.

Maddie pulled the gun out and gripped it tight.

The party ended here and now.

Maddie stepped out and raised the gun at arms length straight out before her.

Chapter 17

He had a reputation for calm, icy authority. Nothing perturbed him. Everything could be worked out. Order and routine were at the heart of everything he did so that he was better able to sow disorder and chaos in the lives of others.

Today that calm was becoming disrupted.

Two men dead and two more in hospital with critical injuries. Bob Willoughby spilling his guts before he could be dealt with. And that young woman he'd been forced to dispose of. Such a mess.

And all because of that woman. Madeline Graves.

He'd done his research, examined every inch of her background. Her life had been laid out before him and opened up. He could find nothing to indicate how dangerous she appeared to be.

But here he was, with two men dead and two badly injured by her hand.

And now she had disappeared.

This couldn't be allowed any longer. He was the expert they brought in to fix mistakes and to clean up the inevitable messes of those mistakes. And yet this time, the situation just kept on deteriorating.

None of it was his fault. They had brought him in too late to dispose of Revel-Humphrey; that snivelling little man had already wreaked damage by contacting Madeline Graves. Those buffoons he'd sent to kill Madeline and her children had been too stupid to double-check their whereabouts, and then they had been upstaged by a couple of brats.

He'd said, after that debacle, he'd told them not to underestimate anyone. Do your job and be professional. Amateurs. He'd assigned the four of them on keeping Maddie and the children in that house until they could find out how much she knew and if she had alerted anyone else. But no, even four of them couldn't seem to keep one woman and two children captive for an afternoon.

And now she was out, and no one knew where. Her options were limited. He had frozen her bank accounts already and later, when this dreadful party was over, he would begin the process of truly eliminating all records of the Graves' existence.

But for now, what remained important was seeing the election night through. Madeline Graves, Jessica and Oliver, they were no longer a threat. How could they be? Nowhere to go, no money, no friends.

What possible danger were they now?

They could go to the police, but there was enough interference spread through the British police force, along with its inevitable bureaucracy, that nothing would be done about investigating her wild claims of a worldwide plot against her. Of conspiracy theories and secret world rulers.

Not tonight, at least, when they had a potential riot on their hands.

No, Madeline would be more concerned with finding shelter and sanctuary. Right now her brain would be reverting to that of a wild animal, one being tracked and hunted. She would be in survival mode.

But he was missing something, wasn't he?

Madeline had a friend. A co-conspirator. She was dead now, but did that mean Madeline was on her own again, or were there others?

He stood at the window and looked out across the City of London, at the Thames flowing powerfully through the city, and at the single boat struggling against the flow.

He didn't like the unknown, the variables.

He was worrying over nothing. Soon the night would be over. The British Values party would be in power, Madeline Graves and her children would be dead.

He turned his back on the window and headed for the noise of the party. Stupid, pathetic morons, celebrating their win before the results were even certified. He stepped into the wall of noise.

What possible danger could there be?

She was one ordinary woman, alone in the world apart from her two children.

Even so, his instincts suggested that he remain alert. Madeline Graves might be a threat still, even now.

But if so, she wouldn't get far tonight.

Chapter 18

Oliver prodded Jessica in the arm.

'What?' she said.

He stared at her, eyes pleading.

They were both sitting on the bed. Jessica hadn't spoken, except to tell him that their mother had gone.

'I told you, I don't know where she's gone.' Jessica looked away.

Oliver prodded her in the arm again.

'Will you stop that?' Jessica smacked his hand off her. 'I don't know what you want. Just speak to me, or write it down or draw me a picture for Christ's sake, I'm not a mind reader.'

Jessica shuffled around, turning her back on Oliver. Her head was filled with the thought of her mum shoving Jessica out of her way, as though she was nothing but an obstacle. Where was she going?

Had she left them? Abandoned them? What were they meant to do now? Stay with the weird guy in the wheelchair?

No. She's coming back. She has to.

There was no way she would have left them here on their own.

But that's just exactly what she did, isn't it? Just walked right on out and shoved you to one side because you were in her way.

Jessica squeezed her eyes shut and balled her hands into fists. This was stupid. She couldn't just sit in this bedroom and wait for her mother to come back. But what else was she going to do?

Look after Oliver.

That was the last thing Jessica's mum had said to her as she left. Jessica looked at her brother, curled up on his side on the bed.

Look after Oliver.

What did that mean? That their mother wasn't coming back? Or had she meant for Jessica to look after Oliver until their mother returned?

But returned from where?

Jessica groaned with frustration.

She couldn't just sit here and wait.

Jessica jumped off the bed and ran out of the bedroom.

'Where's my mother gone?' she yelled.

Alex was cradling a bottle of whisky in his arms. He lifted the neck to his mouth and tipped it back, swallowing noisily.

Jessica approached the wheelchair bound man cautiously. 'Where has my mother gone? Please, tell me.'

Alex lowered the whisky bottle. 'I haven't always been a cripple, you know.' He pounded his fist against his thighs. 'These things carried me once, they had strength and speed. I might as well have them cut off now, for all the good they do me.'

Jessica swallowed a sudden onslaught of tears. She had

to hold herself together. She had to stay composed so that she could find out from this man where her mother had gone.

Alex took another deep swig of the whisky. 'Spider was my legs. She was the one who got out there, took to the streets and found out the shit that I couldn't. And now she's dead. And I'm stuck here, useless.'

'What about my mum?' Jessica kept her voice low and level. 'She could be your legs now. Couldn't she?'

Alex chuckled and whisky dribbled down his chin. 'Your mother's not coming back.'

'What?' Jessica took a step closer. 'Why are you saying that? Of course she's coming back, she has to.'

Alex shook his head. 'Nope.' He reached down behind his back and produced a gun. 'She's gone to kill a few people.'

Jessica let out a little yelp of fear and stepped back. 'Please, don't shoot me.'

Alex lifted his eyes from the gun. Tears had welled up around his eyelids and on the lashes.

'I'm not going to shoot you.' His gaze returned to the gun. 'Not you.'

'Please, please tell me where our mother has gone. Please.'

Without looking at Jessica, Alex said, 'She's on her way to The Shard to kill Edward Porter, and maybe a few other people. She won't be coming back.'

Jessica fled to the bedroom. She dragged Oliver upright and shook him.

'We have to leave right now! I know where Mum is, we have to go to her before she does something stupid.'

Both of them jumped at the sound of a gunshot, followed by the crashing of glass. Oliver clutched Jessica by the arm.

'Stay with me, keep close,' Jessica whispered.

Holding on to each other, they inched towards the bedroom door. Jessica peered outside. The corridor was empty. They padded their way down it and Jessica peered through the next door.

Alex's head slumped forward and his arms hung by the sides of his wheelchair.

'Oh no,' Jessica whispered. 'I think he shot himself.'

Alex's head jerked up, and he lifted the bottle of whisky, which had been hidden from Jessica's view on the opposite side of the wheelchair, and put it to his lips. That was when Jessica noticed the smashed TV monitor.

Drawing Oliver close, she stepped through the doorway. They edged together along the wall towards the exit.

'Where are you going?'

Jessica noticed the gun in his lap. 'We need to find Mum.'

'You shouldn't go out there, it's dangerous.'

It's dangerous in here too. What else are you thinking about shooting up?

'We just need to find Mum, that's all. And then we'll come back.'

Throughout the conversation, Alex hadn't looked at them. He lifted a hand, as though he was dismissing them.

'Go, do whatever you want. I'm not your parent.'

With a flick of her eyes toward the exit, Jessica signalled to Oliver to get out. They hurried silently outside. The door swung shut behind them, and the noise echoed around the concrete stairway.

Rain battered at the window.

The city lights glowed yellow in the distance, the view distorted by the water running down the windowpane.

Jessica and Oliver ran down the steps.

Chapter 19

He noticed it immediately. The shout, the scream, the small scuffle.

Such things were common at a crowded event like this, but that didn't mean it was innocent. He pushed his way through the crowd. He kept his eyes on the centre of the disturbance and ignored the men and women he pushed his way past.

There were three of them, two men and a woman. The woman was wiping at a large, dark stain down the front of her dress.

'What happened here?' he said.

One of the men, all gelled hair and spiky attitude, pointed at the other man. 'This idiot threw his drink everywhere and almost knocked me over.'

'Hey, it wasn't my fault, I was shoved.' Although he protested, his eyes were wide with fear.

'Yeah? Who by, dickhead?'

'Uh, she's gone.'

'Yeah, right.'

He stepped up to attitude man and stared him down. 'You need to be quiet now, and go enjoy the party.'

Attitude man stared back and then dropped his gaze.

'Yeah, whatever.' He walked away.

'Tell me, who shoved you?' he said, turning back to the scared young man.

'I don't know.' He turned and pointed. 'I think she went that way.'

He followed where the young man pointed, forcing his way through the crowd once more. Madeline Graves was here, he was sure of it.

Chapter 20

A MINUTE EARLIER WHEN she had stepped from the stairwell, Maddie had been faced with an empty reception room.

Open double doors led to a conference room. Music throbbing, lights pulsing, a crowd celebrating.

Maddie lowered the gun. Her heart galloped in her chest.

What had she been thinking? There were too many people here for her to barge in brandishing a handgun. What had she planned on doing? Killing everyone?

Maddie slipped the weapon back inside her jacket.

She just had to find Porter. He deserved to die. She had to find him and get him somewhere she could kill the bastard.

He was in there, somewhere amongst that crowd. Partying with the rest of them. All she had to do was find him and get him out of there. Would he recognise her? He must know what she looked like.

Maddie smoothed her wet hair back. She was a mess, looked like a drowned rat no doubt. But it was dark in there, like a nightclub. The darkness, the flashing lights, the party atmosphere, it all might give her just enough of an opportunity to find Edward Porter.

Maddie stepped through the doorway. She was swallowed up by the crowd. Laughter, screams of delight, shouts, singing, the celebrations smothered her. Round tables with white plates, champagne glasses and silver cutlery laid out. Maddie edged her way between men and women, between people seated at the tables, making herself as inconspicuous as possible.

Don't look at me, I'm nobody, no one of interest to you. In fact, I'm such a nobody, I'm invisible.

Two large screen monitors displayed rolling election results. The British Values party were way ahead. If the results continued like this, they would have a landslide victory.

Where the hell was Porter? There was a stage set up at the front of the hall, with microphones on stands. He would announce his victory from here at some point in the night. Probably even before the count had finished. Maybe she could kill him then. She had to get closer; she didn't want to miss.

'Whoa! I love the outfit!'

The man got in close, eyes dulled with alcohol, and placed a hand on her arm. He looked young, not many years older than Jessica, probably. And here he was, out of his depth, trying to be a grownup.

Maddie snatched his collar and pulled him in close. 'Take your stinking hands off me.'

She let go and shoved him. Wide-eyed, he stumbled into somebody and spilt his drink over a woman's dress. She screamed. The man who had been jostled turned and started mouthing off.

Maddie pushed her way through the crowd, away from the disturbance.

This was no way to act. She had to calm down before she made enough of a disturbance that she was noticed. Perhaps it was already too late. Where the hell was Porter?

Maddie paused in her relentless forging of a path through the press of people. She was by a large window and the rain hammered at it, although Maddie couldn't hear it above the music and the chatter. But she could see the raindrops smashing against the glass harder than ever.

In the distance, she saw a brief flash of forked lightning.

The storm, heading their way.

Maddie turned her back on the window and scanned the crowd of celebrants.

There. Edward Porter. All done up like a gorilla in a dinner suit.

Maddie's throat tightened at the sight of him.

None of this made him look respectable. Not the trappings of The Shard, or the suits, or the company he was keeping. He was a thug, a murderer, and nothing more.

He held a drink in one hand and a cigar in the other. He was talking to his right-hand man, Brent Kilburn. Were the two of them ever apart? The thuggish politician and his thuggish minder.

How was she going to do this? She could get in close and pull out the gun, shoot him at close range. Maybe both of them. But then how would she get away? She wouldn't. The crowd would be on top of her before she could escape. She would never see Jessica and Oliver again.

No, they wouldn't. Everyone would scatter at the sounds of the gunshots. There would be a stampede for the exits. That still didn't help Maddie, though.

You're going to die, you know that, don't you? And if by some miracle you manage to finish the night still alive, you're going to spend the rest of your life in jail.

Alex was probably right, but Maddie had come too far now. Two men were already dead by her hands and two more maimed. Spider had died because of Maddie. Perhaps Jessica and Oliver were better off without their mother. Safe, at least.

Kilburn said something, and Porter leaned back and roared with laughter.

She hated him. He deserved to die.

Maddie slipped her hands inside her jacket. The touch of the gun against her fingertips sent a thrill of excitement and fear rippling through her stomach.

Now. Do it now.

Maddie pushed her way through the crowd, working her way towards Edward Porter.

Kilburn spoke once more, and Porter leaned back and laughed again. He slapped Kilburn on the shoulder and handed him the drink. He turned and walked away.

Where was he going?

Maddie followed him.

Chapter 21

That feeling in his stomach, that sense of unease, he hadn't experienced that in a long time. Not since he was a child, after the fire that killed his mother and destroyed the piano.

He'd been taken in by his uncle and aunt. They were elderly relatives of his father with no children of their own, but they had taken their nephew in out of a sense of familial duty. In the first few days following the fire, it seemed that he had an endless flow of visitors checking on him. Family, friends, social workers, the police, all of them concerned for his well-being.

But then, as the days moved on and the investigators suggested that the fire was a result of arson, the flow of visitors slowed to a trickle.

And the visitors left were mostly officials.

The uneasiness intensified as the child realised he was suspected of starting the fire. The questions he answered became less about his welfare and more about the circumstances surrounding the fire. Where had he been? How had the fire started? Why did he not cry?

He stayed calm, despite the roiling nervousness of his insides. All he had to do was answer their questions. Despite how he felt, he knew they would give up in the end.

He was right. Eventually the questions slowed and then stopped, just like the visitors had. But his aunt and uncle never looked at him the same way again. They never showered him with affection the way his mother had. They provided for his needs; food and drink, warmth and shelter, an education.

Nothing more.

Now he was experiencing that sense of uneasiness again. He was the fixer, the one they sent in to clean up messes and fix others' mistakes. He could be relied on. But this situation was like a slippery eel in his hands. Just as he thought he had a hold of it, it shifted and slipped.

Madeline Graves.

A housewife!

How had she managed to inflict such damage and death?

And then there had been Willoughby. What had he revealed in his little chat with Madeline?

Still, Willoughby had been dealt with, although it was unfortunate he'd had to leave that mess with the girl. And now it was election night, and although the Graves woman was still out there, he was sure that she didn't have the full picture yet. She posed no danger to the party's success tonight. They would win the election and tomorrow morning they would be the UK's new government.

So why the feeling of uneasiness?

He pushed his way through the crowd. He was not polite or subtle about it. He didn't care about the sharp rebukes and the protests.

He was growing ever more sure that Madeline Graves

was here.

But he couldn't see her anywhere.

CHAPTER 22

PORTER PUSHED HIS WAY through a door marked 'Gents'.

Maddie hovered outside. This would be perfect. Just the two of them, inside the men's bathroom. But first she needed to make sure Porter was in there on his own. She could wait to see if anybody else came out. But if she waited too long, Porter would finish and leave and she would lose her opportunity.

Maddie touched the gun inside her jacket. It was almost a talisman of good luck. She derived power from it whenever her fingertips brushed against its sleekness.

There was no point waiting. She had to take the chance he was on his own in there.

Maddie pushed the door open and stepped through.

A small dogleg of a corridor blocked her view of the bathroom. She peered around the corner. There he was, standing with his back to her at a urinal. Above the row of urinals was a large window giving views of the Thames and the London Eye and the city beyond. Tonight the view was obscured by the torrential rain hitting the glass.

Porter was on his own. Maddie checked the cubicle doors. They were all open.

Quietly, she walked up to Porter. She withdrew the gun and shoved it in his lower back.

'Stay right where you are. One move and I will shoot you.'

Porter stiffened.

A stream of urine splattered against the tiled floor.

'Put that thing away,' Maddie said.

Porter hurriedly zipped himself up. Dark patches stained his trousers.

Maddie jabbed the gun in his back. 'Over there, in the cubicle. Move, now!'

'Look, whoever you are—'

'Shut the fuck up and do as I'm telling you.'

Porter did as he was told. Maddie followed him to the nearest cubicle, the gun in his back the whole time. She squeezed in after him and shut the door. It was a tight fit.

'Pull your trousers down.'

'What?' Porter was standing at the toilet bowl with his back to Maddie.

She jabbed him in the small of the back with the gun. 'I said, pull your trousers down. Right down, around your ankles.'

Porter fiddled with his belt buckle until it was undone. He pulled his trousers down and let them fall to his ankles.

'Now turn around to face me and sit on the toilet.'

Porter shuffled around until he was facing Maddie and sat down on the toilet seat. The flesh on his face had turned grey and a sheen of sweat sparkled on his forehead and cheeks.

'Do you know who I am?' Maddie said.

Porter shook his head. 'I have no idea.'

'I don't believe you.' Maddie shoved the gun's muzzle into Porter's neck. He swallowed and coughed and banged his head against the cubicle wall as he attempted to retreat from the gun.

'Who am I?'

'I told you, I don't know. Now will you—'

Maddie pushed the gun in deeper into the soft flesh of his throat. 'I'm Madeline Graves.'

Porter's face turned even paler.

'Yeah, you know who I am now, don't you?'

Porter nodded, the movement small, restricted by the gun in his throat.

'Why you, Porter? Why did you do it?'

Porter jerked his head in minuscule movements from side to side.

'What's that? It wasn't you? Too bad there was a witness. That's why my family has been targeted, isn't it? You didn't realise there was a witness until just recently. And when you found that out, you knew you had to get rid of us all. I guess you being our next Prime Minister meant there was no chance for you to get your hands dirty again, right? So you sent those thugs to do your dirty work instead.'

Porter tried to speak, but all he could manage was a tight, hoarse whisper.

'Excuse me? Did you just try to tell me that wasn't you, either?'

Kill him. Kill the murdering bastard now. What are you doing, wasting time talking to him?

Maddie's finger slowly squeezed against the trigger. It would be so easy. All she needed to do was increase the pressure a touch more and the gun would fire. So why was she still reluctant? Why was she wasting time talking to the murdering bastard, questioning him when she already knew the truth?

'Please,' Porter managed to whisper.

Maddie lessened the pressure just a little on his throat.

He sucked in a ragged lungful of air and coughed. 'I honestly don't know what you're talking about. Please, you have to believe me.'

'You know who I am though, don't you?'

Porter nodded. 'I've seen your picture on the news. You killed those men.'

'Yeah, those thugs you sent to murder me and my children.'

'No, no I didn't.' Porter looked like he was about to throw up.

'And Spider, you murdered her too, didn't you?'

'I... I don't know—'

'Stop lying!' Maddie jammed the gun deep into the flesh of his throat again.

Porter gagged and coughed. He lifted his hands and grabbed hold of Maddie's wrist. His eyes bulged.

Maddie squeezed the trigger.

The muffled blast was nowhere near as loud as Maddie had expected. The back of Porter's skull exploded in a spray of red and grey matter. It splattered up the cubicle wall. Maddie flinched at the droplets of warm blood hitting her in her face.

Porter's body sagged and fell forward. Maddie caught him under his arms and held him up. She still held the gun in her hand.

The celebratory noises from the main hall grew louder as the bathroom door opened.

Maddie held Porter's body in place, hugging him where he still sat on the toilet seat. His head lolled to one side, exposing the hole in his skull.

'Ooh, looks like someone's getting his jollies tonight.'

Maddie heard the rustle of clothing and movement just outside the cubicle door. What were they doing? What did he mean?

'Couldn't you two have got a room? That's bloody disgusting.'

Their feet! The men could see her feet along with Porter's, in the gap below the cubicle door, his trousers around his ankles.

Maddie held her breath, concentrating on staying as still as possible. She listened to their movement, clothes rustling, the sound of a zip being unfastened.

'In the toilet as well, it's just not hygienic, right?'

The other man chuckled. 'Maybe he's having a blump.'

'A what?'

'You never heard of a blump?'

'No, and I'm not sure I want to know.'

'It's when you get a blowjob while having a dump at the same time.'

'That is sick.' The sound of zips again, of movement. 'Come on, I can't stay in here any longer. Bloody warped, that's what they are.'

The door opened and closed again.

Maddie propped Porter's corpse against the cubicle wall. When she let go, he began sliding to the side and she had to grab hold of him again. Blood ran in a steady stream from his ruptured skull and onto his shirt. If she left him like this, he would eventually bleed onto the tiled floor. Maddie needed to keep his body hidden for as long as possible. She couldn't let the blood gather and seep out across the bathroom.

Maddie shoved the gun back inside Spider's jacket.

She grabbed Porter with both hands and dragged the corpse off the toilet seat. It slid over the toilet, legs splaying awkwardly either side of Maddie. One of his feet had come loose from his trousers, and now they were gathered around one ankle.

She tried twisting him, turning him around so that he was facing the toilet. If she could just get him so that his head was positioned over the toilet bowl, he would bleed into the toilet water. Porter's big, solid body refused to budge. Maddie bit back a stifled cry of frustration and panic.

She saw one of his feet sticking out underneath the cubicle door.

If someone came in now...

Maddie couldn't let go of Porter or he would slide completely off the toilet seat, and she knew she didn't have the strength to drag him back on. But she had to get that foot back inside the cubicle.

Maddie hooked her foot underneath Porter's leg behind the knee and tried dragging his foot inside. His leg didn't move. She tried again, jerking her foot as hard as she could. His foot shifted slightly, but the movement caused the body to slide further off the toilet seat. The foot slid further out of the cubicle.

Maddie paused, panting as she tried to catch her breath.

Someone could enter the bathroom at any second. She had to pull herself together and get Porter's foot back out of sight.

Maddie heaved at Porter's corpse, angling his torso more centrally onto the toilet seat. His head lolled to one side and blood splattered against the tiled floor. Maddie shoved a knee into his chest to steady his body. Holding onto his shoulder with one hand, she let go with the other and pushed his head back so that the blood dripped onto his chest again.

Now his leg had twisted into an awkward angle and his foot had jammed between the cubicle door and the tiled floor. But with her knee in his torso, jamming him into place, Maddie was able to use her free hand to grab hold of his leg. His flesh was clammy to the touch, the folds of skin around his thigh loose and repulsive.

Maddie pulled at his leg.

The foot stayed jammed where it was.

Maddie dug her fingers deep into the folds of flesh and the tendons in his thigh and pulled again.

Porter's foot came free with a sudden jerk. Maddie's knee slipped. Porter's corpse shifted, its weight carrying it to the floor.

'No!' Maddie hissed.

She clutched at his shirt, but the corpse had picked up too much momentum. Porter's skull smacked against the cubicle wall, leaving a smear of scarlet behind. Now he was sitting on the floor, his legs splayed out. Maddie placed her hand under a knee and lifted his leg up, his foot dragging across the tiles. She jammed her foot against his so that it wouldn't slide back down. She grabbed his other leg and folded that one at the knee so that both legs were bent and his feet were no longer protruding from beneath the cubicle door.

She wrapped her arms around his torso underneath his armpits and heaved with all her strength. The body shifted an inch or two and then she had to drop him back on the floor. He was just too heavy. But she couldn't leave him as he was, his legs would straighten out and his feet slide out under the cubicle door.

The body had to remain undiscovered if she was going to escape.

She wedged herself against his legs to stop them sliding out straight, pulled Porter's trousers over his foot and dragged the belt from the loops at the waist. She wrapped the belt around his legs where they met at his knees, pulled it tight and buckled it up. His legs held in place.

Maddie pulled a length of toilet paper off the roll and wiped up the splodge of scarlet blood on the floor. The toilet paper turned red, staining her fingers. The splodge of blood was now smeared across the tiles.

Maddie dropped the red toilet paper in the toilet bowl and grabbed more. She wiped at the tiles until they were clean and dropped the toilet paper in the water. She straightened up.

A wave of dizziness rushed through her head. Maddie placed her hands against the cubicle wall to steady herself. The dizziness was swiftly followed by nausea. She bent over the bowl and vomited.

Sweat sprang out on her forehead and her cheeks flushed with heat. Maddie waited, head hanging over the bowl. Her eyes flicked to Porter, and the gaping wound in his skull, the hair matted with blood and brain matter.

With another wave of nausea her stomach cramped, and she vomited again.

Trembling, the heat in her body suddenly replaced by a deep cold, Maddie pulled more toilet paper off the roll and dabbed at her lips. She spat into the toilet bowl.

There, you're fine now. You're okay. Just get out of here, get out and back to Jessica and Oliver. You're okay.

Maddie craned her head to look at the gap between the top of the toilet door and the ceiling. Leaving by the door was out of the question. It had to stay locked from inside to keep Porter's corpse from being discovered too soon.

That meant climbing over the top of the door. Could she even fit through the narrow gap, though?

Maddie slipped off her shoes and pushed them under the door. She climbed onto the toilet seat. Looked over the edge of the cubicle door.

Come on, you've got to hurry!

Maddie hoisted herself up and pushed her head through the gap. Her feet kicked the door, her toes slipping off the smooth surface. She got an arm through and hauled herself over the edge. One arm gripping the outer side of the door and her other hand gripping the inside edge, Maddie was stuck. Jammed between the top edge of the door and the ceiling. She kicked her feet out. They smacked into Porter's corpse.

Maddie pushed the flat of her hand against the outside of the door, dragging herself through the gap. She squirmed in the gap, inching her way through until the momentum picked up and she was free. With nothing to stop her fall, Maddie managed to twist so that she landed on her back. She gasped at the impact. She scrambled to her feet.

She retrieved her shoes and slipped them back on. She caught sight of herself in the bathroom mirrors.

Porter's blood decorated her face.

Oh fuck.

At the sink, Maddie flicked on the tap and released a stream of water. She leaned over the sink and splashed water on her face. She pumped liquid soap into her palms and scrubbed at her cheeks and forehead.

The water in the sink turned pink as it circled the plug hole.

Maddie lifted her head and looked at her reflection. Some of the blood spatters had dried on to her forehead. She lowered her face and scrubbed at it with more force.

The music grew in volume as the bathroom door opened.

'I told the silly bastard, you're going to get yourself in trouble that way, but would he listen?'

The music grew muffled once more as the door closed.

'These newbies are all the same, young, dumb and full of—'

They froze as they saw Maddie leaning over the sink, the tap still running.

'Hey, are you okay? You do realise this is the men's toilet, don't you?'

Maddie gripped the edges of the sink and watched the pink water circling and circling the plug hole.

'I know, I'm sorry.' She didn't look up. 'I was sick, I was going to throw up, the men's was closer than the women's.'

The two men drew closer. 'You feeling better now?'

Maddie nodded, still not looking at them. 'A little, yes.'

One of the men walked over to the nearest urinal. Maddie heard him unzip his trousers and then the splatter of urine against porcelain.

'Sorry, but when a man's gotta go, a man's gotta go, right?'

'Don't mind me,' Maddie said.

The water in the sink was running clear now. She turned the tap off.

'Are you sure you're all right?'

The second man, he hadn't moved. He was standing too close.

Maddie nodded. 'I just need a few moments.'

'Can I get you anything? A glass of water maybe?'

Maddie shook her head. 'No, please, don't worry about me, I'm fine.'

'Well, as long as you're sure.'

'Come on, Freddie! Leave the poor girl alone, she doesn't want chatting up right now, mate.'

Maddie heard the man zipping himself up. He walked over to the sinks and stood next to her. He could have chosen any of the sinks, but he chose the one right next to her. He turned on the tap and rinsed his hands beneath the water. Glanced at her.

'Nice jacket.'

'Thanks.' Maddie stared at the porcelain bowl. She could still see faint streaks of pink water.

'Are you sure you're meant to be here? I mean, you know, the jacket's great and all, but it's not exactly appropriate dress considering the event, is it?'

'What the hell, Tom, you just told me to stop chatting her up and now you're interrogating her. Leave the poor girl alone.'

Tom turned off the tap. 'I'm just asking, that's all.' He shook water off his hands.

'My boyfriend is here, I just dropped him off. I wanted to have a look before I left so I came up with him and then I felt sick.'

The man held his hands motionless over the sink. 'You drove your boyfriend into central London?'

'No, I came with him on the Tube. He hates public transport, it gives him anxiety attacks.'

'Yeah?' He obviously didn't believe her. 'You want me to go get him?' He picked up a paper towel and began drying his hands.

'No, it's okay. I'll be out in a second.'

'It's no trouble. What's his name?'

'Honestly, please...' Maddie held in her scream of frustration. 'Please, I just need a few moments on my own.'

'Come on, Tom, leave her alone. Let's go.'

'You had your piss yet?'

'Nah, I don't need one anymore.'

Tom screwed up the damp paper towel. 'I hope you feel better soon.'

'Thank you.'

Maddie held her breath until the two men had left and the door had closed behind them.

'Shit, shit, shit, shit, shit, shit. Oh fuck, shit, fuck.'

Maddie straightened up and gazed at her reflection. Strands of hair were plastered across her face. Bloodshot eyes. Pale complexion, like a ghost.

Maddie dried her hands on a paper towel.

She had to get out of there before Tom decided to come back and question her some more.

Chapter 23

Sometimes he wondered if he had a sixth sense.

All his life he had been able to sense trouble, to detect bullshit, like an early warning system. This feeling had become a part of his armoury. His tools of the trade, as it were.

Like that time in Vienna, at the Heiligenkreuz Abbey. If not for his intuition, he would have died that day. Instead he survived, and the two men sent to murder him lost their lives in his place.

Now that early warning system was on full alert, and yet still he had no idea why. He'd searched the entire floor of The Shard, and he could find no trace of Madeline Graves. And yet he was convinced she was here.

He glanced at the large screen monitor. The British Values party had raced so far ahead in the results they were now guaranteed their place as the UK's next government. As always, he had been asked to step in and rescue a rapidly deteriorating situation and he had done so. His reputation remained intact. He could return home now and wait for the next contract.

And yet...

He couldn't ignore that sixth sense of his. A lifetime's

experience had taught him this.

Relax, he told himself. He took a slow, deep breath, concentrating on the sensation of his lungs filling with air and then emptying again. *Don't think, just concentrate on the breathing. Empty your mind of everything else and simply breathe.*

There. He saw it, out of the corner of his eye.

He pushed his way through the crowd once more, focused laser-like on Brent Kilburn and the man talking with him.

'What's going on?' He looked at the other man.

'Tom says there's a woman in the men's toilets.'

Kilburn was saying something else, something about Porter having visited the toilets and not returned, but he wasn't listening. He headed straight for the bathrooms.

What an idiot he'd been.

Chapter 24

Had Jessica ever seen so many people crammed into one place before? Not outside of a pop concert, she hadn't. That had been exciting, but this was terrifying.

Jessica gripped Oliver's hand as she darted through the gaps in the crowd, the sudden openings between bodies that lasted only a matter of a second or two before closing again. A downpour pounded their heads and shoulders. Jessica thought the rain would have dampened the protesters' spirits, but if anything it seemed to be fuelling their anger.

Not my government!
Not my government!

The chants echoed off the buildings. Protesters waved placards and held up banners. The rain poured off their faces and flattened their hair to their scalps. Jessica had overheard someone saying that there had been clashes with the Alphas on the Southbank. That the police presence there had lost control and that soon reinforcements would be arriving with teargas and water cannons.

Jessica wanted her mum more than ever.

They needed to find her before she did something stupid, something... terrible.

The faces of the crowd were suddenly lit up as a bolt of lightning seared its way across the cloud filled sky. Moments later and thunder pealed directly overhead and some of the crowd screamed.

Oliver pulled at Jessica's hand. His eyes were round and wide with fear.

'I know, I know, but we've got to find Mum.'

Where was The Shard? When they had climbed the steps out of the tube station, Jessica had seen the signs. It hadn't been far to walk. But now, trapped in the middle of this mob, Jessica could no longer see any signs and didn't know if they were still headed in the right direction. She looked up at the skyline, searching for its distinctive profile, glowing bright against the night sky. But they were hemmed in by too many buildings, and she couldn't find it.

The Shard had to be close. It just had to be.

Dragging Oliver with her, Jessica continued pushing her way between close-packed bodies.

A space opened up and Jessica dashed for it. She just needed a moment to breathe, to pause.

Railings obstructed their way. The Thames flowed fast and high, the lights of the surrounding buildings reflected and distorted on its dark surface.

'We've gone too far!' Jessica turned her back on the Thames. There was The Shard, its glowing tip pointing at the sky.

Oliver wrapped his arms around Jessica's torso.

'It's okay.' She hugged him tight. 'We're almost there, look. I know where to go now.' Rainwater ran down her face and dripped from her nose and her chin. 'Let's get moving and then we can get inside and be out of this rain at least.'

She felt Oliver's head nodding against her shoulder.

Lowering their heads, the two children began forcing their way through the packed crowd of protesters once more.

Chapter 25

Maddie pulled open the toilet door and stepped into the hall.

Walking towards her, the man stared straight at her.

She had been discovered.

Maddie turned to run in the opposite direction and stopped. There was one more door, marked Ladies, and then the corridor finished at a fire escape door. Maddie spun around to face the man headed her way.

She pulled the gun out of the jacket.

Thunder rolled overhead as a flash of lightning lit up the windows. For the tiniest of moments, the scene was frozen in time. The man advancing upon her; the party happening behind him. Even Maddie seemed frozen, her hand which just a moment ago had been reaching for her gun, now completely still.

Someone screamed. A ripple of nervous laughter ran through the crowd.

The lightning died away.

Before she had a chance to bring the gun up, the man was on her. A hand grabbed Maddie's wrist, yanking her arm up, twisting it. A grunt as the man tried to snatch the gun from her hand. Maddie kicked out and her foot connected with soft tissue. A yelp, and the hand let go of her wrist.

Another rumble of thunder and bursts of lightning.

The black silhouette of a figure, outlined against the lightning flashes, lunged for Maddie. He smashed into her, knocking the gun from her hand.

'Where is Porter, Madeline? Where is he?'

Maddie jabbed at his face, hoping to plunge her fingers into his eyes. The jab glanced off the side of his forehead. She grabbed his ear and twisted it.

He yelled and punched Maddie in the stomach. Maddie doubled over as her stomach exploded in agony. Multi-coloured lights dazzled her, dancing around in her vision. Hands grabbed her, pinning her against the wall.

Maddie twisted and writhed in the man's grip, trying to break free. She snapped her head forward, anything to try to make contact, deliver a punch or blow.

Nothing.

'Stop fighting me! Where is Porter? What have you done with him?'

The man glanced back at the party in the conference hall. Still pinning Maddie to the wall, he twisted and glanced at the toilet door marked Gents.

He pulled Maddie away from the wall and shoved her towards the restroom door. He bent down and picked up the gun Maddie had dropped.

Maddie strained to take one last look at the victory party still happening in the conference hall. A door had been closed on the corridor. The sounds of people chattering, laughing, the music, filtered through the door.

None of them knew what was happening. Help

wouldn't come.

The man jabbed the gun in her stomach and grabbed a fistful of her hair. Dragging Maddie with him, he pushed open the door and stepped inside.

The bathroom door closed behind them.

The man let go of her hair and pushed her away. She tottered backwards until her bottom hit the row of sinks. She placed her hands against the cold, hard edge.

The man extended his arm and pointed the gun at her. 'Stay right there.'

He picked up a tall stool with a vase containing a spray of dried flowers on it and jammed it against the door to the restroom.

Maddie watched him as he turned and looked at the cubicle door, the only one closed of the three cubicles in the bathroom. He lifted a foot and kicked the door in.

The door jammed against Porter's body, sprawled over the toilet and dripping blood.

'Oh fuck!' He turned to face Maddie and his upper lip curled back as he delivered a punishing punch to the side of her head. 'Fuck! Fuck!'

Maddie's legs buckled. She tried to hang on to the edge of the sinks, but crumpled slowly to the floor.

The man kicked her in the side. Maddie rolled over as her world disappeared into a fiery chasm of agony. The red hot, burning pain radiated from her side and through her torso, down her arms and legs and up into her head. It crawled into every fibre of her body, seeking out places to express itself where she had never hurt before. It was like a living creature, sent to torment her.

'You fucking stupid bitch!'

The man kicked her again, this time in the lower back. Maddie screamed as the previous pain dissolved into nothing compared with this whole new agony. Her vision greyed out, and a high, whistling in her head drowned out all other sounds. Even the pain faded away for a brief moment, before all her senses rushed back at her, overpowering her with their need for attention.

Maddie gasped, sucking in air as her body attempted to deal with this sudden agony.

The man stood over her. Maddie had never seen such hatred in a face before as she saw in his now. He reached out a hand to her. It seemed to be growing in size, becoming this huge, monstrous hand that grabbed her by the jacket and lifted her up.

Before she got far another hand appeared, this one bunched into a fist. Maddie turned her head away, and the fist smashed into her left cheekbone. Her head snapped back with the force of the blow. The man let go, and she fell back to the floor.

The man said something she couldn't catch. The voice echoed down to Maddie from high above. She was lying in a deep pit of agony, but the distant voice came to her from a place where there was no pain, somewhere she had been once.

Maddie opened her eyes, sticky with blood. She could taste the warm blood on her lips. The high-pitched whistling had ratcheted up a notch. It seemed to be piercing bone and flesh, cutting through her brain. Maddie blinked her eyes, trying to clear the blood out. She couldn't see properly. Looking at her hand lying on the floor just inches from her face, it was as though she was looking at it from behind a layer of gauze.

She blinked once, twice. Her vision cleared in her right eye, but she was blind in her left, where the man had punched her. She didn't need to touch it to know that the left side of her face had swollen up.

She lay on the floor, her cheek against the cold tile, and watched the man's feet as he walked back and forth, back and forth, in the restroom. He stopped walking, and the feet changed direction and stepped over to Porter's corpse.

'Fuck.'

'He deserved to die,' Maddie said, her voice thick, and the words slurred.

The feet turned, the toes of the black shoes pointing at her, like twin cannons ready to fire on her. Maddie wanted to roll her head back, look up and see his face. It just seemed like too much effort.

The feet stepped closer. Strangely, the man seemed calmer now. Maybe it was the gun in his hand, enabling him, giving him power over her.

'What did you say?' He took another step closer, the tips of his shoes almost touching her ruined face.

Maddie worked some saliva into her mouth and tried again, louder this time. 'I said he deserved to die.'

'And why was that?'

Even though he spoke without raising his voice, Maddie heard every word he said. He seemed more in control now than he had a minute ago.

Maddie gathered her energy to speak again. The act of choosing words and forming them into sentences was incredibly difficult at that moment.

'He murdered my husband, and Harry, my little boy. He

sent thugs to murder me, but they killed my sister and they kidnapped my children. He deserved death.'

'Oh, really? What gives you the idea that Mr Porter murdered your husband?'

'I know he did. I have proof.'

He squatted in front of her. 'What proof?'

Maddie tilted her head slightly until she could see his face. 'Who are you?'

He cocked his head to one side, as though thinking. 'I don't suppose it matters if I tell you, does it? I am Krystopher Kreadey, also known as the Ghost.'

'Why... why are you doing this?'

'It's my job, it's what I am good at and known for.' He lifted the gun and pointed it at her in a casual, off-hand way. 'But you, young lady, you're making my job very difficult. I've got quite a mess to clean up here, haven't I? And that doesn't bode well for my future employability.'

Maddie licked her lips. Her tongue felt sticky and swollen. If she could just keep him talking until someone tried opening the door to the restroom, they might go and report it.

'I don't understand.' Her words slow and slurred.

'Never mind that.' He waved the gun in her face. 'Now tell me, what proof do have that Mr Edward Porter murdered your family?'

Maddie closed her one good eye. The floor seemed to be tilting beneath her, and she expected that at any moment she would begin sliding along it.

'My son saw him, saw him kill my husband and his little brother, he saw it all.'

Kreadey chuckled. 'Is this the one who doesn't speak?'

'His name is Oliver, and he doesn't speak anymore because of the trauma of seeing his family murdered.'

Kreadey sighed, as though he had the weight of the world upon his shoulders. 'It really wasn't supposed to happen that way. I suppose I was distracted. You see, I usually work on my own.'

Maddie kept her eyes closed. Perhaps if she lay here long enough, she might go to sleep, and just slip away into nothingness. Leave behind all the pain and the anguish. But Kreadey's words niggled at her. Something he'd said...

'What... what do you mean?'

'Edward Porter didn't kill your husband and child, Madeline. I did.'

Maddie opened her eye, blinking away sweat and sticky blood. The tips of his shoes were only inches from her face. The left shoe had a smear of red blood on its tip.

Kreadey was telling the truth, Maddie knew that even though she wished he was lying. Somehow Oliver had got himself mixed up, mistaking Kreadey for Porter. But how? The two men looked so different.

Kreadey chuckled. 'Little Miss Vengeance comes to get revenge, and what does she do? She kills the wrong man.'

No, Maddie realised. Oliver hadn't been wrong, he hadn't mixed the two men up. Porter had been there; he was the man in Oliver's drawing wearing the tie. Kreadey had been the one holding the knife dripping with blood.

'Porter was there when I disposed of your husband, but he was a bystander, an observer. He was a weak man, and he needed to see the consequences of betrayal.'

'Why did you have to kill Harry? He was only little.'

'I know, Madeline, I do. I know my job is killing people,

but believe me, I'm not a monster. Your little boy was in the wrong place at the wrong time. If it's any comfort at all, I did it quickly.'

Maddie clenched her teeth.

'Now, Madeline, where are Oliver and Jessica? Are they nearby?'

'They're nowhere you will ever find them.' Maddie spat the words out.

'Well, let's not worry about that right now, shall we?' Kreadey stood up. 'Dear me, what a mess you've made, young lady. I should really be making you clear it all up, but that's not practical right now, is it?'

Kreadey grabbed Maddie by her jacket and pulled her up to a sitting position, leaning her back against the wall.

'Why are you doing these things?' Maddie said.

'It's my job, I told you.' Kreadey picked a heavy marble dish off the sink and smashed it against the mirror. A crack ran through the glass, like the lightning bolt they had seen minutes before. Kreadey smashed the dish into the mirror again and several shards dropped into the sink.

He picked one up.

He hadn't taken his eyes off Maddie once.

'Hold out your arms.'

Maddie shook her head, her lank hair whipping across her face. 'No.'

'This will go easier for you if you do as I say.'

'Why should I make it easy for you? You're going to kill me.'

'No, you're going to kill yourself.' Kreadey held up the sliver of glass. 'You're going to slit your wrists open and bleed out all over the floor until you're dead.'

'It won't work, there will be too many questions. And how are you going to get Porter out of here without anybody noticing?'

'I don't need to.' Kreadey smiled. 'You will be found with the gun you used to murder Porter in your hand. Your injuries will be explained away by Porter trying to defend himself. You killed him and then in a fit of despair you committed suicide.'

'I'm not going to make it easy for you.'

'I didn't expect you would.'

Kreadey advanced upon her.

Behind him the mirror's cracks suddenly spread, and the glass fell in pieces into the sink and across the bathroom floor. Kreadey spun around in surprise.

Maddie fell on her side amongst the shards of glass. Her hand found a long sliver and closed around it. Blood seeped between her fingers as she lifted the glass shard. The pain meant nothing to her, it was barely noticeable beneath her raw nerve edges, still screaming in agony at the kicking Kreadey had given her.

Maddie dragged herself upright, and sliced the glass sliver in a broad arc at Kreadey. He staggered, slipping on tiny glass fragments crunching beneath his shoes, and fell. The gun flew from his hand and skidded across the tiled floor.

Kreadey jumped to his feet and reached out to grab hold of Maddie. She plunged the point of the glass sliver through the flesh in the palm of his hand. He screamed and snatched his hand away.

Maddie stabbed at him again, but Kreadey backed up, clutching his wounded hand to his chest. She thought he might keep backing away, but instead he lunged for her again. This time he managed to grab Maddie's wrist and force her hand, holding the weapon back, twisting her arm. Ignoring the pain, Maddie shoved herself against Krcadey and sank her teeth into his ear.

He didn't scream or cry out at all, but his grip on her wrist lessened and Maddie was able to twist it free of his hold. She plunged the glass shard at his side, but he blocked her arm with his and grabbed her hair with his other hand. Maddie released her bite on his ear and clamped her hand over his face, pushing him back.

Kreadey let go of her hair and they both stepped back, panting heavily. She flicked her eyes between Kreadey and the restroom door, holding the shard of glass out and daring him to come for her. Blood dripped from her hand, hitting the floor in steady drops.

Where had the gun landed? If only she had a chance to search for it. Maddie knew that as soon as she took her eyes off her attacker, he would be on her.

Maybe it was time to get out. Get outside amongst the people celebrating. What would he do then, this killer? How would he explain this away? All the blood? The dead body of their party leader?

Kreadey would blame her, of course. And with the police already after her in relation to the attack on the Mulvaney family, what kind of defense did she have?

'What are you going to do now, young lady?' Kreadey eyed her warily. 'Make your move.'

Maddie blinked blood from her eyes. No good, her vision was blurred. But she could see Kreadey well enough. Keeping him in view, Maddie backed up towards the bathroom door. Whatever she did right now, she was in trouble. But if she got out of here, at least she might live.

Maddie reached behind her, and her hand found the handle on the door. She kicked the heavy vase blocking the door out of the way.

Still holding the shard of glass out at arm's length, she stepped back through the doorway. The door swung closed and Maddie turned and ran.

Chapter 26

When Maddie stepped back into the party, she had expected all eyes to turn on her. Maybe someone would scream, there would surely be gasps of horror and surprise. And then what? Would people back away? Would anyone rush to her aid? Not likely while she was still holding that long, pointed shard of glass, the blood dripping from her hand.

None of that happened. As Maddie pushed her way through the door and back into the party, all eyes were fixed on the large screen monitors. A cheer erupted around the room. The election was still hours away from being called, but the British Values party was so far ahead that victory was inevitable.

Maddie forced herself to move. If she could get out of here while they were all distracted, if she could just get to the lifts, past the security guards and out of The Shard...

'That woman murdered Edward Porter! Stop her!'

Kreadey's ragged yell cut through the party atmosphere, silencing the room in moments. And now every eye turned upon her. Maddie froze, holding the glass shard straight out in front of her, the blood dripping in a steady stream and hitting the floor with a splat.

'Stay back!' Maddie hissed. 'Stay back, all of you!'

She cast a quick glance at the exit. It was so far away, between tables piled high with food, chairs pulled out, and people, so many people. Maddie looked back; Kreadey was pushing his way through the crowd.

Maddie started backing up to the exit, swinging her arm in a wide arc as she moved. Apart from Kreadey, no one moved.

Her thigh bumped against a table and she shuffled around it. A woman, eyes wide and mouth trembling, backed away as Maddie drew closer. Maddie risked a glance over her shoulder. The exit was closer now, but still so far away, and so many people between her and her escape route.

A hand grabbed her wrist. The man was middle-aged and fat, but his grip was strong. He propelled her back with his bodyweight until her thighs hit a table and she was forced onto her back. She dropped the shard of glass as she skidded over plates of food and drinks, scattering them to the floor.

'I've got her, I've got her!' He was panting with the exertion and his breath stank of stale cigarettes as he leaned his bulk on top of her.

Maddie's free hand scooted through the debris on the table, trying to find purchase, to stop herself sliding across the table top. Her hand closed around a fork.

With a roar, Maddie swung her arm in a powerful arc and plunged the fork into the man's ear.

He screamed and let go of her wrist, his weight shifting as he grabbed at the fork and yanked it out. Freed from his bulk pinning her down, Maddie picked up a plate of half-eaten food and smashed it in his face. She snatched a silver kebab skewer off the table, chunks of chicken and peppers still attached to it. Wrapping her arm around the man's neck, she pulled him close and pushed the sharpened tip of the skewer against his throat.

'Everyone back off.'

The man grabbed her wrist and tried to pull her hand away from his neck.

'Stop that, or I will shove this in deep in your throat.'

His hands fell away.

Maddie started backing up, pulling the fat man with her. His weight sagged against her, as though he had lost all his bravado and had gone weak at the knees.

'Stand up!' she hissed.

The room was silent, and the rain pounded against the floor to ceiling windows. The horizontal edges of the windows glowed with a soft blue light, and outside the darkness was punctuated with the glow of the city lights.

Maddie couldn't make out anything specific beyond her immediate vicinity. The vision in her one eye was still blurred, like someone had smeared Vaseline over a lens.

But she could see Kreadey, matching her pace whilst he kept a reasonable distance from her.

The man was panting and snorting.

'He's having a heart attack,' someone said.

'No.' Maddie glanced over her shoulder at the exit.

'Let him go, he needs medical help.'

The man's weight had grown heavier against her and he began sliding down her front no matter how hard she tried to keep a grip on him.

She pushed him away and turned and ran for the exit.

Felt like she was shuffling more than running. Every bone in her body protested with bolts of agony as she forced it to move.

She pushed through the doors to the reception, leaving smears of blood across the glass. There, the elevators. She limped toward them.

She hit the button to summon the lift. Glanced back and saw Kreadey heading for her. She pushed the button again, jabbing at it. No good, it was taking too long.

'Don't come any closer.' Her voice sounded thick and muffled, like she was slurring. Still clutching the kebab skewer in her fist, Maddie edged away from the lift.

Kreadey paused, keeping a wary eye on the skewer.

'You can't keep this up forever, Madeline,' he said, drawing out the vowels in her name. 'You look about ready to fall over any moment.'

'I'm going to kill you. I'm going to kill you.'

Kreadey held up his hand and showed her the ripped flesh in his palm, the edges pink and raw.

'You already tried.'

Maddie's back bumped against a set of double doors. She pushed her way through.

'You can't come in here, Miss!'

Gleaming metal worktops and cookers ran in lines down the long kitchen. Men and women in white uniforms dashed between each other, calling out instructions. Steam filled the air, the sound of sizzling competing with the raised voices.

Maddie jostled her way past the kitchen staff, holding the skewer out like a sword.

'Everyone, out of my way.' She turned back the way she

had come.

Kreadey had pushed his way through the door but pulled up short.

The kitchen staff backed away.

Kreadey picked up a knife from a counter top. 'Now Madeline, are you sure you want to do this? A knife fight?'

'I killed your men, in that house.' Maddie thrust the skewer at him, even though he was beyond her reach.

'That was impressive, I have to say. But you were lucky. You can't count on that luck again, Madeline.'

The kitchen had emptied of staff. Maddie was on her own with this man.

Kreadey smiled and rotated the wide knife from one side to the other, allowing the steel to flash in the kitchen light. 'Madeline, Madeline, surely you must see that your position is hopeless. My job is killing people, it's all I do, and you seriously think you can fight me and survive?'

'What choice do I have? You're going to kill me, anyway.'

He turned the blade over again, the light flashing on its mirrored surface. 'This is true, but if you let me, I can make it quick.'

'And then what? You'll hunt my children down and murder them too?'

'I told you Madeline, I'm not a monster. I don't want to kill your children.'

Maddie lunged and thrust the skewer at him. Kreadey knocked her arm out of the way and sliced his knife across her front, slashing through the jacket.

A scream ripped from Maddie's mouth. She smashed into Kreadey, knocking him against a pan of boiling water. It toppled from the cooker, the clang as it hit the floor reverberating through the kitchen. The boiling water splashed across the tiles and Kreadey leaped out of its way.

Somehow Maddie had lost her weapon. She scrambled for Kreadey's arm, fending off his attack as he plunged the knife at her face. Maddie knocked his arm out of the way and they both stumbled against the cooking range.

Kreadey screamed as his hand landed on the flames of a gas hob. He snatched his hand away, dropping the knife so that he could cradle his injured arm. He glared at Maddie, sweat running down his face, his eyes narrowed with hatred.

Maddie backed away, between grills and more cooking ranges. The kitchen heat had become oppressive. Pots on stoves were bubbling and Maddie could smell meat burning under grills and in pans.

Kreadey straightened up. He tilted his head, cricking his neck.

A griddle pan burst into orange and red flames beside Maddie. The flames shot up to the exhaust system, and the opening erupted into flames. With a soft explosion, a deep-fat fryer showered bright, flaming spots of oil across the kitchen.

Kreadey bent and picked up the knife.

The wail of the fire alarm cut through the kitchen and water sprayed from the ceiling.

Kreadey's eyes glittered in the glow of the fires around the kitchen.

Maddie picked up the flaming griddle pan and flung it at Kreadey. He staggered as the griddle pan hit him in the chest, and screamed. The pan hit the floor, spilling its flaming contents across the tiles.

Maddie backed further away from Kreadey. His outline shimmered in the heat as the fire began spreading between Maddie and her pursuer. Smoke poured from around the edges of an oven door. Orange flames spread across the ceiling, shooting from one vent opening to another.

Kreadey was no longer visible, separated from her by a wall of fire.

Maddie limped deeper into the kitchen inferno. Sweat ran down her face and neck. Were the doors that she had entered the kitchen through the only exit? She seemed to be in the heart of the fire now, with no escape. Even if she had the strength to make it through the fire back to the kitchen entrance, Maddie doubted she could find her way.

But she had to. She had to get out of here, back to her children.

No, wait, she had to find Kreadey. She had to make him pay for what he had done.

She spotted a wide, gleaming carving knife lying on a chopping board. She closed her hand around the handle and picked up the knife.

A cloud of dark, greasy smoke rolled towards her along the underside of the ceiling. Still clutching the knife, Maddie dropped to her hands and knees. The floor had grown warm, almost hot beneath her.

She crawled on, looking for an escape.

Chapter 27

Kreadey backed out of the kitchen as sweat poured down his face. He dropped the knife before he pushed his way through the door and back outside the kitchen. The fire alarm's insistent wail cut through his head like a steak knife slicing open his brain.

Turning his back on the kitchen, he held up his hand to inspect the damage. Skin had begun peeling away, but the flames had at least seared the wound that woman had inflicted upon him with the shard of glass. No one had caused him this much pain before.

No doubt there was a service elevator for the kitchen. He hoped she found it and escaped from the conflagration. Kreadey hated the thought of her dying in that fire. He needed her to live so that he could take pleasure in killing her slowly when he caught her.

Kreadey punched the button to summon the lift. Thankfully, these modern buildings had elevators that continued to work even in fire situations.

The lift doors slid open and Kreadey stepped inside. Looked like he was the only one left on this floor. The lift doors slid closed, and the elevator began its rapid descent.

There was a service and delivery area around the back of

The Shard. If Madeline managed to escape the fire in the kitchen, that was where the lift would deposit her.

And Kreadey would be there to meet her.

Chapter 28

The fires had sucked all the oxygen from the kitchen and left Maddie crawling across the floor on her belly like a snake. A hacking cough had replaced the act of breathing. Her throat felt scorched, like it was on fire. Tears dripped from her eyes, stinging with the heat and the smoke.

All she could do was slither along the floor, between stainless steel industrial kitchen units. She had no idea where she was going. No destination in mind. All that was left was to move, keep moving as long as she was able to.

She hit a dead end. The wall rose before her, disappearing into the black, boiling cloud of smoke. Maddie turned to the left and began crawling alongside the wall. It opened out to her right. Her fingers found a gap in the floor, a straight line following the route of the wall.

It was an elevator, its doors wide open.

Maddie crawled inside. The floor was utilitarian, scratched and scarred over years of work. She was in a service elevator.

But would it work? Weren't elevators designed to stop working in a fire? And yet, here it had been, waiting with open doors for her to crawl inside.

Maddie climbed to her knees and reached up. Her fingers found a column of ridged buttons. She pushed the bottom one.

The lift doors slid closed. Maddie slithered down the lift wall and sat on the floor. She cradled the carving knife against her torso. The elevator began its descent. Maddie's chest heaved as she coughed. The air in the lift was thick with greasy smoke. Beads of sweat ran into her eyes, stinging them. Her head throbbed with pain and her left eye felt like it was protruding from her skull. She still couldn't see anything from it.

The elevator slowed to a halt. Maddie climbed to her feet as cool air flowed in between the opening doors. Steadying herself with her uninjured hand, Maddie limped out of the elevator compartment. The rain pounded steadily at the ground, but Maddie was sheltered in a delivery parking space. Concrete walls and iron girders stretched out before her, vans parked in bays, all illuminated by overhead lighting.

Thunder rumbled overhead.

What now, Maddie?

Get back to her children, that's what. She'd come out here bent on vengeance, filled with hatred and a vicious anger, and still she had failed. The wrong man was dead, and the bastard who had murdered her son and husband was still out there.

But she had to get back to Oliver and Jessica. And then flee. Maybe Alex would help her. He might be able to get them new identities, they could move to another country, start again.

Or maybe not. Maddie had no idea who Alex was or how far his skills and influence stretched.

And perhaps Maddie should simply accept the inevitable, and hand herself in to the police. What kind of life would it be for Jessica and Oliver, on the run, constantly looking over their shoulders, hiding from the law?

Still clutching the knife, Maddie limped into the delivery bay. A light flickered overhead. She walked between white vans. The pounding of the downpour against the street grew louder as Maddie approached the exit.

'Hey, you can't come in here.'

Maddie froze, hidden between the vans.

'This isn't a public entrance, man, you can't come in here.'

Was he speaking to Maddie? She couldn't see anyone.

'I'm sorry, I must have taken a wrong turn.'

Kreadey! He was here already, waiting for her.

A young black man in a security guard outfit stepped into view in front of Maddie. He was standing side on to her at the front of the two white vans. Maddie held her breath.

He pointed. 'That's okay, just head back up there and round to the left, and that'll get you to the main entrance. Nobody's getting in tonight though, the upper floors are being evacuated.'

'Oh dear, I hope it's nothing serious.'

'It's a fire, man, least that's what I heard.' He stepped out of Maddie's view, closer to Kreadey, she assumed, who she could not see.

Maddie heard a gasp, and the van next to her rocked as though something had hit it.

Maddie backed away. At the rear of the two vans she turned and ran as softly as she could. She crouched and limped behind a line of parked cars. She caught a glimpse of Kreadey between concrete pillars, lowering the body of the young man he had murdered to the ground.

Maddie kept moving. Kreadey was turning his head, searching for her. He began walking deeper into the service bays. Slipping the knife into her jacket, Maddie ran out of the service area and into the rain. Water began streaming down her face and her neck. She limped towards the flashing blue lights illuminating the darkness.

At the front of The Shard's entrance, a paramedic ran towards her, but Maddie pushed him away.

'I'm fine.'

'No you're not, let me take a look at you.'

'There are injured inside, they need your help.'

The paramedic pointed to an ambulance. 'Go over there, they will attend to your injuries.'

He left, and Maddie limped on. Ignoring the ambulance, she peered into the night and the rain. She could still see nothing from her left eye, and her right had limited vision. Her world was a dark blur.

'Mum!'

Maddie's heart jumped at the sound of Jessica's voice. A mixture of joy and despair. What was she doing here?

'Jessica?' Her voice was a thick, slurred mumble. 'Jessica?' Louder this time.

'Mum!'

And there she was, running to her, with Oliver in tow. Jessica pulled up short when she saw her mother properly.

'Oh my God, what happened to you?'

With her good hand, Maddie pulled Jessica close and then Oliver. 'I've had some problems, but I'm okay.' Her speech was still slurred.

Oliver pulled away and tilted his head to gaze wide-eyed at his mother.

'It's okay, it's all going to be all right, but we need to get out of here now.'

'You should go to hospital,' Jessica said.

'Not now, later.'

Jessica wiped wet hair off her face. 'But look at your hand, and your face. What happened?' Her eyes welled up with tears.

Maddie pushed at her children, encouraging them to move. 'There's no time, we have to go.'

Firemen ran past them. Another ambulance arrived. People were still flowing out of The Shard's entrance and being guided away. Maddie glanced up at the tower, its lights glowing against the darkness of the cloudy night sky, and blinked as rain hit her face. She could see no sign of the fire from out here.

They allowed themselves to be herded along with everybody else. Maddie's head throbbed, the pain notching up a level now that her mind wasn't so preoccupied with an immediate threat to her life.

Still, they had to get a move on. But where to? Who could she trust? The only family she'd had was her sister Ellie, and she was dead. What about Martin, Ellie's husband? No, she couldn't drag him into this. And besides, his solution would be to contact the police.

Maddie didn't know if she could trust the police.

Maddie glanced back over her shoulder. She couldn't see well enough to tell if Kreadey was following them. She thought about asking Jessica to take a look for her, but decided against it. Maddie didn't want to alarm her children any more than they already were.

The rain battered her, stinging her cuts and broken nose, the water running into her eyes. She had to blink to keep her vision as clear as possible. People stared as she shuffled past. Maddie knew she must look a sight with her bruised and bloodied face, strands of wet hair hanging from her head, and her awkward, painful gait.

Maddie decided to forget about finding a destination at the moment. She just had to concentrate on running. Up ahead she could see lights. Her vision was too blurred for her to read the illuminated sign, but she knew where she was; London Bridge Underground.

Oliver tugged on his mother's hand. His eyes were like saucers. He lifted a hand and pointed behind them.

Kreadey. Oliver had seen Kreadey. Maddie glanced back, but still her blurred vision kept her from seeing him.

She bent down. 'Run. Go in the underground, get on a train.'

'But... we don't have money for tickets.'

The hitch in Jessica's voice cut through Maddie like a spear. 'Climb over the barriers, but you have to run now.'

Oliver bolted for the Underground entrance. Jessica stared tearfully at her mother, and then she ran too.

She pulled up short just inside the entrance to the station and looked back.

Maddie waved her on. 'Go! Stay with Oliver!'

Jessica ran. Maddie followed, grateful to be sheltered from the rain battering her.

She saw Oliver scrambling beneath a turnstile as an overweight member of staff shouted at him. Jessica scrambled over the top of the turnstile and dashed after Oliver down the steps to the underground.

Maddie hoisted her aching, bruised body over the barrier and fell to the floor on the opposite side. More shouts of protest.

Maddie ignored them.

Fresh bolts of agony shot through her body. She climbed to her feet and shuffled down the steps.

More shouts above her. Screams. A distant rumble.

Whatever was happening, Maddie ignored it.

She got to the bottom of the steps where the tunnel split into two. Eastbound or Southbound.

Maddie took a chance and headed for the Southbound platform. With her peculiar, hopping, running gait, Maddie passed posters advertising West End shows, new films, art exhibitions. The brick ceiling curved over her like a tomb.

Maddie spotted Jessica waiting at another junction.

'This way!' She turned and ran.

The rumble of an approaching train. A rush of warm air. The squeal of brakes.

Maddie rounded a corner and there was the tube train, doors sliding open, men and women spilling from it like cattle set free from the transporter.

Ollie! Maddie caught a glimpse of him on the platform before he was swallowed up by the crowd of commuters and tourists. Where was Jessica?

The train began filling with people and the platform emptying.

Oliver looked over his shoulder and spotted his mother. Maddie waved him on, urging him to board the train before the doors closed. Oliver stepped inside.

'Mum!'

Jessica grabbed her mother's hand. They dashed across the platform and boarded the train just as the *Doors Closing* alarm sounded.

The doors slid shut, and the train began moving. The platform slipped by and then they were in the tunnel, the windows black. Oliver was in the next carriage along and Maddie kept her eyes fixed on him, just visible to her through the tiny windows in the doors separating them.

Jessica stood beside her mother in silence.

The train began to slow, and they exited the tunnel, pulling to a halt at a platform. Blackfriars.

Maddie shuffled up close to the doors separating the carriages. She grabbed the handle and twisted it, and the door swung open. The gap between the doors was narrow and Maddie reached out and opened the next door.

Jessica followed her and closed the door.

'Excuse me, but are you all right?' A middle-aged woman, looking up at Maddie from her seat.

'I'm fine,' Maddie said.

She shuffled down the aisle, between seats filled with people. Her thigh and her back throbbed where Kreadey had kicked her. Her skull vibrated with a hot burst of pain where he had punched her. Had she ever felt this exhausted? This beaten?

'Mum!' Jessica hissed. 'There's a man following us.'

Kreadey.

The doors slid shut, and the train pulled out away from the platform and back into the darkness of the tunnel. Maddie gripped a handrail as the carriage rocked from side to side.

They had to get off the train at the next stop. But how far could they run? Maddie was in no condition to keep running, and she couldn't fight him. And even if Jessica and Oliver ran and escaped, he would find them eventually.

And he would kill them.

Maddie had to stop him. She had to finish this now.

With a squeal of brakes, the train slowed to a sudden halt. Passengers rocked in their seats. The momentum almost carried Maddie over.

Someone sighed and muttered something about delays. The tinny sound of music turned up loud and played through earbuds. Someone coughed twice. The rustle of a newspaper as the large sheets were turned over.

A distant rumble, just on the edge of Maddie's hearing. Growing louder.

'What's that noise?' A young woman, her head cocked as she listened.

The tannoy crackled into life. 'Please will all passengers take their seats. The underground is experiencing some severe flooding. Please stay seated.'

The tannoy fell silent.

That low rumble, growing in strength.

The floor began vibrating, the sensation travelling from the soles of Maddie's feet and up her legs.

'Oliver! Hold on, hold on tight!' Maddie grabbed Jessica. 'You too.'

Oliver gripped the pole with both hands. The vibration grew stronger. An old man yelled and stood up. The woman next to him pulled him back down into his seat.

The rumble had become a living thing that surrounded them. Maddie could no longer work out where it was coming from. It seemed to have engulfed them, swallowed them whole, and now they were in the belly of a beast, and the rumble was the workings of its stomach and its digestive system.

The carriage shunted forward as something slammed into it. The movement threw Maddie off her feet, and she smacked into the carriage floor, pulling Jessica with her.

The carriage lights flickered, but stayed on. Maddie heard the tannoy burst into life with white static, a panicked voice behind the buzz shouting something incomprehensible. Men and women screaming, a rush of bodies.

'Oliver!' Maddie screamed. 'Oliver!'

Jessica had fallen on top of her mother. She placed her hand on the carriage floor to push herself upright. A man stepped on her hand as he clambered over her, and Jessica screamed in pain.

Another massive jolt slammed the carriage, and the floor and the walls trembled with the force.

Maddie heard screams from another carriage and a window smashing.

She dragged herself up onto her hands and knees. Jessica helped her.

'Where's Oliver?' Maddie could see only blurred bodies scrambling for safety down the carriage.

'I don't know, I can't see him!'

Maddie saw thin jets of water shooting from between the rubber strips where the train doors met.

The tunnel was flooding.

Maddie climbed unsteadily to her feet. The tube train

passengers were bunched up in a crowd down at the other end of the carriage.

Jessica yanked at her mother's hand. 'Mum, I heard someone say the front carriage is at the next platform.'

Jessica pulled her mother with her, and they stumbled down the aisle between the empty seats. As the carriage trembled beneath the force of the water shooting through the tunnel, passengers fought to push their way through the door into the next carriage.

'Oliver!' Maddie yelled from the back of the packed group.

Jessica pounded her fists on the backs of the people in front. 'Get out of our way!'

More passengers stumbled down the aisle behind Maddie and Jessica, pushing them into the packed bodies in front. Hands clawed at Maddie, hot breath fluttered against her face. Screams, sobbing, panicked yells.

Suddenly the blockage of people broke, and the doorway cleared. Jessica had been right, the next carriage along had managed to get to the next platform. The passengers were pouring through the open door and onto the platform, splashing their way through ankle deep water.

Holding onto each other, Maddie and Jessica stumbled onto the platform. Maddie snapped her head from side to side as she searched for Oliver. There were too many people, a crush of bodies rushing for the stairs, to the exits leading above ground. Trying to escape before they were drowned like rats in the tunnels. And Maddie could only see through the one eye, and even that was blurry.

More screams, but this time from the exit. Bodies tumbling down the steps leading up to the next level. Arms and legs tangling with each other as more water cascaded down the steps. Behind Maddie the train groaned and then shunted forward as a second powerful surge of water slammed into it from the tunnel.

'There he is!' Jessica screamed. 'Oliver! Ollie!'

Maddie looked where Jessica was pointing and waving. She couldn't see him.

'Take me to him,' she said.

They had to fight their way through the panicked people milling about on the platform. Water poured across the platform and cascaded over the edge and onto the track, slowly filling it and turning it into a canal.

Still Maddie couldn't see her son.

No, there he was, jostled and pulled this way and that by the crowd.

Maddie reached out to him.

A body slammed into her, driving her through people and down to the ground. Kreadey's leering face hovered over her, drawing in and out of focus. Water poured over Maddie, and she coughed and spluttered.

Kreadey grabbed Maddie by the jacket collars and hauled her upright. He dragged her to the edge of the platform and shoved her off it. The floodwater level had reached just below the lip of the platform, and Maddie disappeared beneath the surface.

The gritty, oily water invaded her mouth and nose and throat. Her hands found the hard edge of the track, the rough surface of the wall, and then she was out. Coughing, choking, her wounds stinging.

She couldn't see. Just blurred shapes, moving shadows.

Why was no one helping her? Where were her children?

The sound of water splashing beside her. Fingers snagging her jacket, hands closing around her arm.

Had someone jumped into the water to rescue her?

With a powerful thrust, the hands shoved Maddie into the swirling, filthy water. She screamed, and it turned into a choke. Her hands flailed at Kreadey with a life of their own. Fingers clawing at him, reaching for his face, searching for his eyes, for soft meat that she could pierce with her fingernails.

Kreadey pulled her to the surface. His crazed eyes fixed on her.

'There's a reckoning coming, Maddie,' he yelled. 'A reckoning.'

Maddie clawed at his face, but then she was under the water again, coughing and choking. Her feet kicked at the ground, catching on the rails. She flailed at Kreadey, but she had no control over her limbs anymore.

Kreadey dragged her to the surface once more. He shoved his face up to hers and it was all she could see in the flickering lights of the station.

'It doesn't matter if you die today, or tomorrow, or next week.' His lips curled back in a snarl. 'We're all just passing time, just waiting for that day when we will pay for our misdeeds. I'm doing you a favour, killing you now. But your kids? Oh, I think I will let them live, so they can suffer along with everybody else.'

Kreadey shoved Maddie beneath the water's surface again. Above it, a thundering reverberated along the platforms and through the tunnels. The force of it made the water shiver, and Maddie felt it coursing through her body. It didn't matter, nothing mattered anymore. All she wanted was one final breath of clean air, but a few moments from now even that desire would disappear.

The kitchen knife.

Maddie had hidden the knife in Spider's jacket. Her hands clawed for it, her fingers snatching at the handle. She withdrew it from its hiding place as Kreadey pushed her weakened body deeper into the filthy water. With the last of her fading strength, Maddie blindly shoved the blade at Kreadey.

Even beneath the surface of the water, Maddie heard him scream. The knife was torn from her weak grip as his body jerked away. His hands let go of her.

Maddie fought her way to the surface. She sucked in the stale, warm tunnel air and coughed. Water poured off her head and down her face. The coughing racked her body, sending spasms through her chest. She vomited water up and coughed some more.

'Mum! Mum!' Jessica, standing with her in the water.

'Where is he?' Maddie's voice was no more than a strangled croak. She whipped her head from side to side, looking for Kreadey. She could hardly see anything, just dark, blurred shapes.

No, there he was, wading chest deep through the water, away from Maddie and her children. He was clutching his stomach.

Maddie followed him.

'Mum, no!' Jessica yelled.

Ignoring her daughter's cries, Maddie hauled herself through the water. As if sensing her presence, Kreadey glanced back over his shoulder.

Maddie reached out and her fingers snagged his collar.

With all the fading strength she could muster, she dragged him back and down. Kreadey disappeared beneath the water for a moment. When he fought his way back up, he was coughing and spluttering.

He smacked her across the face with a wild swing of his arm. White hot agony swept through Maddie's skull. Her knees buckled beneath the force of the pain. Kreadey was wading through the filthy water, towards the dark tunnel opening.

Maddie ground her teeth together, willing the pain away. She pushed after Kreadey. He had to die.

'Mum!' Jessica screamed. 'Don't leave us here!'

Maddie ignored her daughter. Kreadey was all that mattered now. His murder.

'Mum!'

Maddie pushed on, her body and mind consumed with a murderous rage.

'Mummy!'

Maddie halted. An electric charge seemed to have flooded through her.

Oliver?

Maddie turned. There he was, kneeling on the platform, one hand held out towards her. Tears streamed down his face.

Maddie glanced over her shoulder to see Kreadey swallowed up by the tunnel's darkness.

She let him go.

Helped by her children, Maddie clambered up onto the platform. They were shin deep in water now, but the torrent of water down the escalators had slowed to a gentle waterfall.

They were the only ones left on the platform.

Maddie pulled Jessica and Oliver close and hugged them like she would never let go.

Chapter 29

The rain stopped, and the skies cleared of clouds. A full moon hung over the City of London, but nobody paused to gaze at it in admiration. Emergency crews worked through the night, rescuing victims of the Thames flood, pumping water out of the underground stations, pulling dead bodies from the wreckage of trains.

The news of the flood battled for the top spot with that of Edward Porter's murder. The British Values Party's victory in the election became a side item to the main drama.

After Maddie and her children had made their way back to London's surface, they were taken to hospital. In the confusion and the mass of flood victims needing medical attention, Maddie's wounds did not stand out as remarkable. Maddie had taken a battering when the floodwaters hit, and she was lucky to be alive.

Her eye was bandaged up, she was given strong painkillers and an appointment with the Ophthalmology Department for the following day.

'Make sure to keep this appointment,' the nurse said. 'That eye needs to be checked out properly.'

Maddie nodded.

Her body ached with the need for rest. For sleep.

Held by Jessica and Oliver, Maddie limped out of the hospital. She called a taxi, and when she was asked her destination she paused, unable to think.

Where was there to go? Who could help her now?

There was nowhere. No one.

Maddie and Jessica and Oliver were on their own.

Except, maybe there was one place to go to. One person who might help.

Maddie pounded her fist on the door. There was no buzzer or intercom beside the keypad, which unlocked it. Maddie rested her forehead against the door and closed her eyes. Climbing the flights of concrete steps up here had almost finished her off. If she didn't sleep soon, she thought she might go crazy.

Jessica shook her mother's arm. 'Mum, there's a camera in the ceiling. He must know we are here.'

Maddie nodded. 'I'm sure he does. Maybe he just doesn't want us here.'

'Or maybe he's dead.'

Jessica had told her mum about Alex and his gun and how wild with grief he had gone. It had already occurred to Maddie that Alex might have put the gun to his head and pulled the trigger. In which case, they truly were on their own.

Oliver slipped his hand into Maddie's and she squeezed it gratefully. Her head throbbed and her eye felt as though it might explode from the bandage covering it. Every spot where Kreadey had kicked and punched her was on fire right now, and her bandaged hand pulsed with pain where she'd had stitches.

Maddie flinched at the sound of the click. The door sprung open an inch.

Jessica pushed at it.

The door swung open onto the empty hall, the broken lift to their right and the door at the opposite end. Automatic lights came on.

With her children beside her, Maddie limped through the hall to the next door.

Jessica opened it.

Alex was waiting for them. 'Come in.'

Maddie paused on the threshold of the door. 'Are you...?'

'I'm fine.' Alex nodded at Jessica. 'Honestly, I'm fine.' He turned his attention back to Maddie. 'Come in, you should get cleaned up, get some rest. We've got work to do.'

'What work?'

'We need vengeance, Maddie, for Spider's murder, for everything you have been through. We need justice.'

Maddie nodded. That sounded right.

Justice.

Acknowledgements

As always I need to thank Carrie Rowlands for being my 'first reader'.
If she doesn't like it, it doesn't get published!
Thanks also to my advance reader team for your reviews.

JOE COFFIN

Vampires on a murder spree.

A hitman out for revenge.

How hard can it be to kill the undead?

While Joe Coffin served his time in prison, someone spilled his family's blood. But when the massive hatchet man takes out the killer, something about his vengeance feels completely off. He never expected his suspicion would reveal corpses sporting the marks of a ruthless vampire. As local children start to disappear, Coffin teams up with an ambitious reporter to get to the bottom of the deadly mystery. Out of his depth against a supernatural powerhouse, he's unsure any amount of killing could've prepared him for the fight. But he's willing to put it all on the line when he discovers his wife and son might not be as dead as he first thought...

Can Coffin stop the carnage before more bloodsuckers rise from the grave?

Joe Coffin, Season One is the first book in a brutal vampire thriller series set in the British underworld. If you like hardcore characters, page-turning suspense, and gory crime mysteries, then you'll love Ken Preston's supernatural horror thriller.

kenpreston.co.uk/

Joe Coffin Chapter One

Jacob Mills' best friend, Peter Marsden, had been begging him for months to break into Ninety-nine Forde Road with him. He said maybe they would find a dead body in there, or maybe they would meet a ghost, or get chased by a zombie.

None of these things particularly appealed to Jacob, but Peter kept on and on at him, wearing him down, bit by bit.

The dilapidated Victorian house had been empty for as long as they could remember. Every morning, as they walked past it on their way to school, they'd tell each other stories about ghosts wandering through the deserted rooms and corridors, skeletal hands clawing at the bannisters as they shuffled down the stairs, blood dripping from their empty eye sockets. That's how Jacob wanted it to stay, a house they visited only in their imaginations.

The house had been constructed of odd angles and weird extensions. Over the years, sections of it seemed to have sunk slightly, giving the rambling, pointed structure an even more unsettling appearance. Dark windows of different shapes and sizes sat uncomfortably with one another, some of them so recessed under the eaves it was difficult to imagine how they could receive any natural light.

Vines trailed all across the frontage, around the weathered window frames and over the front door. Even the tall, tottering chimney pots were being slowly strangled by long, green fingers. Jacob was half convinced that one day he would walk past, and the house would be gone, completely hidden by a mound of twisted greenery.

A set of wide stone steps, chipped and discoloured from years of neglect, led up to the front door. Two stone gargoyles guarded the steps, squatting on pillars, their fat lips set in permanent sneers, baring their teeth at anyone foolish enough to approach them.

Jacob could never imagine himself walking past those gargoyles, fearful that they would spring to life, and pounce on him, sinking their stone teeth into his stomach and ripping out his guts.

The two ten-year-olds lived a few streets away, in River View Gardens, a rundown housing estate, notorious for the number of jobless who lived there. The estate had been built seven years ago, its architects promising it to be a bold new experiment in mixed social housing. Now the bigger, more expensive houses lay empty or occupied by squatters, whilst the smaller houses were rented out mostly to single mothers and the unemployed.

In all the time that Jacob had lived in River View Gardens, he had never found a river there, or anywhere nearby.

Jacob and his mother and father had moved into a tiny box of a house on the estate when he was three years old. When he was eight, his father came home drunk one afternoon, and flew into a rage over nothing, it seemed to Jacob. His father had picked up a plate and hurled it across the tiny kitchen where it smashed against a wall. And then he had picked up another, and hurled that one, and another, and another. Jacob's mother had been washing up at the kitchen sink, and she stood there helpless with fear, soap suds dripping from her hands held up in front of her face.

When he had finished hurling plates and mugs, Tom vented his fury at his wife. Jacob had hidden under the kitchen table, sick with fear and shame, and watched as his father punched and slapped his mother around the head. When she fell to the floor, he began kicking her in the stomach.

Jacob had finally crawled out from beneath the table and rushed at his father, beating him on the back, and screaming at him to stop kicking his mother. Jacob's father had ignored him, probably hadn't even realised he was there, and only stopped when he heard the police pounding on the door, alerted by the call of a distressed neighbour.

The police found Jacob's father standing over his wife, his chest heaving as he sucked in great gulps of air, his fists clenched and his face contorted in anger. Jacob's mother lay curled up on the floor, tiny rivulets of blood running across the floor from beneath her head.

The police arrived and arrested Jacob's father for assault. Jacob had only fragmented memories of that day, but he had gleaned enough knowledge over the years to work out what happened.

Jacob's mother refused to press charges, but the police prosecuted anyway. Jacob wondered why they bothered. They knew his father was part of the Slaughterhouse Mob, and sure enough, Mortimer Craggs supplied the best lawyers money could afford, and Jacob's father walked free.

Jacob had never thought his mum would take him back in again, but she did. He soon realised she couldn't afford not to. Jacob's father spent the next few months creeping around the house, trying to ingratiate himself with his wife and son. Jacob wondered what was going on, until he heard his mother talking to Steffanie one night, telling her how Craggs had leaned on Jacob's father, told him to keep his temper in check from now on. Said if anything like this happened again, Craggs would let Joe Coffin loose on him.

There was no mistaking what that meant.

Jacob was scared of his father, and greeted his awkward attempts at befriending him with sullen, monosyllabic replies. It was only a matter of a few days before the father gave up trying to make peace with his son, and they existed in the same house without talking to one another, and by keeping out of each other's way.

Peter lived at the other end of the estate, in a house pretty much identical to Jacob's. Peter's mother always had a cigarette dangling from her mouth, or held between two fingers. When she finished one, she immediately lit up a second. Even outside, playing, if Jacob got close enough to Peter, he could smell the stale cigarette smoke on his clothes, and in his hair. Jacob once heard his mother and her neighbour, Doris, talking about Peter's mother. Doris said she was a slut, and Jacob's mother agreed. Jacob wasn't entirely sure what a slut was, but he knew it wasn't a nice term. He thought about telling Peter, but decided against it.

Both boys were small for their age, but the similarity ended there. Peter was thickset and bullish, like his mother. Jacob was slim built, and much quieter.

Peter had already explored the overgrown grounds of Ninety-nine Forde Road with his best friend, Dougie. They had found a cellar door at the rear of the house, which had probably once been used for coal deliveries. The wood of the door was rotten, and Peter had been able to pull soft chunks of it free with his fingers, surprised woodlice scuttling over his hands and dropping to the ground.

The two friends had hatched a plan to break into the house, one day in the summer holidays. The trapdoor was padlocked, but the clasp was loose in the rotten wood. Peter said they could easily wrench it free. But then Dougie's family had moved away suddenly, and Peter had no desire to go exploring the rambling old house by himself.

Who knew what grisly horrors might confront him, once inside, and alone.

So he worked on Jacob, telling him the house was surely deserted, had been for years, and there was nothing to worry about, Peter would look after him. Jacob was reluctant and took some persuading. It was autumn, the leaves turning brown and falling from the trees, before Peter convinced him that breaking into Number Ninety-nine was a good idea.

One Saturday afternoon, whilst Jacob's mother was out at work in the local supermarket, and Peter's mother was 'entertaining' a man friend in her bedroom, the two boys climbed over a fence at the rear of the house and dropped into the long, brown grass of Number Ninety-nine. The sky was overcast and the light dull. Already, at two o'clock in the afternoon, it appeared night was creeping up on them.

Jacob's insides were loose with excitement and nerves. The boys crouched beside an enormous ash tree, its dying leaves making a dry, rustling sound in the light breeze. They stared at the house, at its murky windows, their filthy net curtains already conjuring up images of ghosts in Jacob's head. Part of him wanted to run, and yet the windows, like monstrous eyes, captivated Jacob, and challenged him to venture inside and discover the house's secrets.

The two boys crept closer, until they were near enough that they could see the vague, shadowy shapes of furniture through the patio windows.

"I'm not sure I want to do this," Jacob whispered.

"Don't be a pussy!" hissed Peter. "You'd better come into that house with me, or I'm telling everyone at school that you're a queer!"

Jacob knew it was no idle threat. He followed Peter through the long grass and stingers, holding his hands up by his chest so he wouldn't get stung, and approached the cellar door.

The clasp had been wrenched from the rotten wood, and it lay beside the trapdoor, the padlock still attached to it.

The two boys looked at each other.

"Did you do this?" Jacob said.

Peter shook his head. For once he seemed to have nothing to say.

Peter bent down and lifted the door open, propping it against the wall.

Jacob looked nervously at the stone steps disappearing into the gloom. He could hear the traffic rumbling along Forde Road, and some young kids playing hopscotch in a nearby street. Outside the grounds of Number Ninety-nine, life was moving on as normal. But here, time seemed to have stopped. Even the leaves had stopped rustling in the wind, and there was no sign of the rats that the residents of the estate backing onto the house complained of so often.

"Let's do it, then, yeah?" Peter said, his voice small and insubstantial, not his usual brash tone.

The two boys pulled torches out of their pockets and shone them down into the cellar. Thick strands of dusty cobwebs clung to the dank stone walls, and Jacob's torch light caught the movement of startled spiders, scurrying into gaps between the stonework.

Peter stepped carefully through the cellar opening first. He hesitated on the top step and turned, his eyes round and wide, to look at Jacob. As though perhaps willing his friend to call the entire thing off, and Peter wouldn't call Jacob a faggot, or tell anybody at school about their cowardice. The look only lasted a moment, before Peter began walking down the steps. As small as he was, he had to duck his head as he descended.

Jacob watched his friend disappearing into the dark. He thought about turning and running, leaving Peter to face whatever was in the house, alone. He could sprint back and climb over the garden fence and be back in the safety of his own house in no time. Even the thought of having to endure Peter's taunts of 'Faggot!' and 'Pussy!' on Monday morning, didn't seem too bad right at that moment.

He had endured worse over the years.

But something in the darkness of that house called to him. The mystery that lay behind those blank windows appealed to him, in some grotesque, twisted way.

He stepped through the cellar opening, and followed his friend, descending into the black underbelly of the house.

Rivulets of dark, oily water trickled down the uneven cellar walls. As Jacob crept through the cellar, he realised his feet were getting wet. He pointed his torch at the floor.

"Peter!" he whispered. "Watch out for all the puddles."

"How did all this water get in here?" Peter said. His voice wavered in the dark. He sounded nowhere near as confident as he had when he first talked about breaking in to Number Ninety-nine.

"I think it must be seeping up through the floor." Jacob bent down and touched what he thought was a dry patch of ground. His fingers came away damp and dirty.

"Look at that, somebody's been digging a hole down here!" Peter pointed his torch at a large, black shadow on the cellar floor.

Jacob approached it, shining his torch in the same direction. The hole was about six foot deep, and long and wide enough it looked like a grave. There was an empty wooden box inside, like a coffin, stained a dirty, dark brown.

Beside the hole lay a sledgehammer and a spade, and a mound of black earth.

Behind the hole in the further reaches of the cellar was a collection of ancient stone jars, scattered haphazardly over the floor, their lids by their sides.

Peter swung his torch around. "Bloody hell, look at that!"

Illuminated in the diffuse circle of torchlight, Jacob

saw a pair of rusted jaws sitting on the floor, their teeth snapped shut, and pointing up to the ceiling. The two boys approached it with care, fearful that the jaws might open up and snap their legs off.

"What is it?" Peter whispered.

"I think it's a mantrap," Jacob whispered back. "They were used for catching poachers a long time ago. If you step into it, it springs shut, and cuts off your foot."

"How do you know?" Peter said, scornfully.

Jacob shrugged. "I dunno. I think I heard about it in a history lesson, or something."

"Look over there, I bet that leads into the house."

In the pale light, Jacob could see a set of narrow steps disappearing up into the gloom. Stepping carefully past the large hole in the ground, Jacob and his friend walked slowly over to the bottom of the steps. They pointed their torches up, the combined light cutting through the darkness to reveal a closed wooden door at the top.

The two boys looked at each other.

"What do you think?" Peter whispered.

Jacob knew that his friend had lost all his bluster and confidence. At that moment, he could have said that he wanted to go back, and he knew Peter would agree. There would be no name calling at school, no taunts of 'Faggot!' That Peter had not had the guts to explore the house, either, would be a secret to be kept forever, a bond between them as powerful as if they had.

This was Jacob's moment, when he could back out of their plan with no shame.

But his friend's bluster and name calling outside had stung Jacob. A perverse desire for revenge festered in his mind.

"I think we should stick to the plan," Jacob said. "You're not scared, are you?"

"'Course not," Peter hissed. "I'm not a bloody queer, you know."

Peter took the steps first. Jacob regretted riling his friend and losing his last chance to back out without losing face. Whatever happened next, he was sure Peter would insist on exploring the entire house.

"Come and help me," Peter said, pushing at the door.

Jacob joined him on the top step and the two boys pushed their shoulders against the old, heavy door, and shoved. It gave a little, and then some more, in tiny, juddering increments. The bottom edge of the door scraped against the floor, leaving curved trails of filth in its wake.

Once they had created a big enough gap, they slipped through, and into a narrow passageway. Uneven slabs of stone formed a floor of sorts, and the walls were whitewashed brick. After all the noise they had made, as they had forced the door open, the silence was shocking and oppressive.

On their left was a second door. Jacob peered through the dirty glass panes.

"This leads back outside," he whispered, hoping his friend would suggest that they use it and escape.

"There's another door down there," Peter said, pointing with his torch. "Let's see where it goes."

They crept down the passage, and Peter pushed open the door. They entered an enormous kitchen. The torch light rambled across wooden counter tops filled with broken plates and bowls, scattered silverware, and mounds of what looked like black ash. In the middle of the kitchen, there was a massive table.

Jacob's torchlight strayed across the table, its surface dark with stains.

Jacob stared at the table like it was something completely alien to him. His lips had gone dry, and his tongue suddenly seemed too big for his mouth.

Jacob pointed his torch up. Hanging from the high ceiling, above the table, were rows of meat hooks. He shuddered a little at the sight.

The two boys left the kitchen and walked down the narrow passage and through another door. Now they were in the reception hall. In the silence of the house, Jacob could hear a lorry thundering by on the main road. But it sounded distant, as though the lorry was on the other side of town, or an echo from a different time.

In the weak light struggling through the filthy windows, they could see a broad staircase sweeping up to a galleried landing.

"Let's have a look upstairs," Peter whispered.

All Jacob wanted to do was make a run for it out of the front door.

He followed Peter up the stairs.

There were several doors on the landing, all closed apart from one at the rear of the house. It was open just a crack, and Peter headed straight for it. Jacob could see the beam of his torch shaking as he walked.

It was no surprise when he heard Peter whisper, "Let's just look in here and then get out, yeah?"

"Yeah, I've got to get back," Jacob said.

"Me too," Peter replied. "Mum will be wondering where

I am."

They were both lying, and they both knew it. It didn't matter anymore. They had crossed a threshold together, and neither one of them would grass on the other one for being scared.

Peter pushed at the door, and it opened easily and silently. Jacob was standing right behind him. Heavy curtains, hanging over the window, blocked out the last of the daylight. There was a big, old wardrobe standing in the corner, and a chest of drawers with ornate handles. Fat church candles sputtered and flared, puddles of wax gathering around them, where they sat on the floor. Greasy, black smoke curved upwards from the orange flames.

Jacob and Peter stood in silent terror, watching the man and woman on the bed in the flickering light of the candles. They were naked; the man lying on his back, his cock swollen and stiff. The woman was straddled across his chest. She had wrapped both her hands around his head, and she was thrusting her hips against his face, buried in her groin.

Her flame red hair cascaded in curls over her shoulders and down her back as she arched her head, her mouth open, as though she was about to scream.

Peter dropped his torch. It landed with a dull thud on the carpet.

The woman snapped her head around, tendrils of her hair falling across her face. She stared at the boys as she continued gyrating her hips against the man beneath her, pinning his head between her legs. His hands were on her buttocks, his fingers digging deep into her flesh.

The woman stared at Jacob, smiling slyly as she rocked

back and forth. Jacob felt as though he was retreating deeper and deeper into his own mind, searching out the recesses and the hidden places, somewhere he could hide from this hypnotic, terrifying spectacle. But whatever he tried, her eyes followed him, penetrating into his most secret places and laying them bare.

A pink, pointed tongue flitted out of the woman's mouth, and she licked her upper lip, all the while still staring at the boys.

Peter screamed.

The spell was broken. Shocked out of their torpor, the two boys turned to run. Peter tripped and stumbled against the door, and it slammed shut. Jacob grabbed the handle, but the door wouldn't move, as though it was now part of the wall, as though it had never been opened at all.

Jacob heard movement behind them. Peter had already turned around, putting his back against the door. His eyes were wide and round, tears brimming over his lower lids, and he was mouthing words that Jacob could not hear.

He turned around. The woman had climbed off the bed. She was staring at them as she walked towards them, her movements slow and languid, like she had all the time in the world.

Her red curls, flowing over her shoulders, and the red triangle of hair between her legs, were a shocking contrast to her white, unblemished skin.

As was the dark red blood, running down the insides of her thighs.

Peter was sobbing, his face a blotchy mess of tears and snot. Jacob pushed at the door again, but still it refused to budge. The woman slowly licked her top lip again as she drew closer. Hoarse, throaty laughter filled the room. In the candlelight, shadows flickered over the walls, seeming to dance along with the mad cackling.

Like a lithe cat suddenly tiring of its game, the woman pounced on Peter. She dragged him to the floor, straddling him like she had the man on the bed. Peter screamed, pounding at her naked chest, sobbing helplessly. The woman gazed at him, her tongue running along her top lip.

She grabbed his hair and yanked his head back, exposing the soft flesh of his throat.

Jacob looked away as she fastened her teeth on his friend's neck. Jacob wished he could block out the other boy's sobs, the sound of teeth tearing at flesh, and then he flinched as heard something snap, and Peter's screams turned into a wet gurgling and sucking gasp.

When Jacob looked back, he saw the naked man sitting up on the bed. His lips and teeth were smeared with the woman's blood, and it dribbled from his mouth, as he watched the woman huddled over Peter's limp body.

Jacob, realising he had been pushing at the door, pulled instead, and yanked it open. He tumbled outside and sprawled across the landing. As he scrambled to his feet, he glanced back and saw through the open door the woman feeding on his friend, sucking at the wound in his throat. The man crouched beside the woman, lapping like a dog at a gathering pool of blood on the floor.

Jacob ran for the stairs, his legs trembling and threatening to fold up beneath him with every step. Half running, half falling, he made it to the ground floor and ran for the cellar. The light was fading fast now, and he had left his torch upstairs where he had dropped it in his terror.

He stumbled down the passage, not daring to look back, even for an instant, and plunged headlong into the pitch black of the cellar. His feet slipped on the steps and he fell out of control. His shoulder hit the stairs midway down, and then his head cracked against a step as he tumbled to the cellar floor.

Struggling to his feet, Jacob blinked warm blood out of his eyes. His hands were dripping with mud where they had landed in a puddle, and his head felt like someone had plunged a knife into it. But, even in his pain and terror, a small, rational part of his mind warned him to be careful of the large hole in the ground, and the mantrap.

Holding his hands out in front, Jacob shuffled cautiously forward in the dark.

Up ahead he saw a faint glow of grey against the total dark of the cellar. It was the open cellar door, leading outside, to freedom. Forcing himself to walk slowly and carefully, he headed for it. Once outside he could dash through the overgrown garden and leap over the fence, and then he would be safe. The first house he got to, he would pound on the door, beg for help. Maybe Peter was still alive, maybe it wasn't too late if the police came now.

Jacob got to the trapdoor and scrambled up the steps and into the garden. In the late afternoon darkness, he could just about pick out the massive ash tree, and the fence behind it.

Stumbling towards freedom, long tendrils of grass grasping at his ankles, Jacob struggled not to burst into tears. If he started crying now, he knew he would collapse, and the monsters inside the house would have him.

He paused by the tree, leaning against the trunk, and steeled himself for the run across the last few yards, and then the scramble over the fence. He took several deep breaths, trying to calm himself.

A sudden blow from behind shoved him face down on the ground. Before he could scream, he had been flipped over on his back and a bloody hand clamped over his mouth. The woman's long tendrils of hair tickled his face as she leaned over him, her mouth smeared with blood.

Jacob tried biting her hand, struggling beneath her weight, but it was no good.

She leaned closer, her tongue slithering out of her sticky mouth, strings of red saliva hanging from her sharp teeth.

The terrified boy snapped his eyes shut, waiting for the sharp bite of her teeth in his neck.

Writing in the Shadows

Would you like daily, bite-sized pieces of fiction delivered straight to your inbox?

Writing in the Shadows is a newsletter for readers who can't get enough stories to feed their voracious appetites. It's also for readers who live hectic life-styles, and would love flash fiction and serialised stories just long enough to read on the way to work, or in a snatched few minutes in the day.

Check out some of the editions here, and then sign up.

https://writing-in-the-shadows.ck.page/